Clamor
of the Lake

Clamor
of the Lake

Mohamed El-Bisatie

Translated by Hala Halim

The American University in Cairo Press
Cairo   New York

English translation copyright © 2004 by
The American University in Cairo Press
113 Sharia Kasr el Aini, Cairo, Egypt
420 Fifth Avenue, New York, NY 10018
www.aucpress.com

First published in Arabic in 1994 as *Sakhab al-buhayra*
Copyright © 1994 by Mohamed El-Bisatie
Protected under the Berne Convention

First paperback edition 2008

Dar el Kutub No. 14767/08
ISBN 978 977 416 241 1

Dar el Kutub Cataloging-in-Publication Data

El-Bisatie, Mohamed
        Clamor of the Lake / Mohamed El-Bisatie; translated by Hala
    Halim.—Cairo: The American University in Cairo Press, 2008
            p.   cm.
            ISBN 977 416 241 2
            1. Arabic fiction   I. Halim, Hala (trans.) II. Title
            892.73

1 2 3 4 5 6 7 8   14 13 12 11 10 09 08

Designed by Sarah Rifky
Printed in Egypt

Translator's Acknowledgments

First and foremost, I wish to express my gratitude to Mohamed El-Bisatie for his unfailing good cheer and faith in the translator. I thank editor Hosam Aboul-Ela for his astute suggestions, and for his receptiveness to my different approach to translation. Michael Heim, translator and professor of Slavic Languages and Literatures, University of California, Los Angeles, generously helped me put the last touches to *Clamor of the Lake*, in keeping with his adage that "God is in the details." This translation brought me in contact with artist Moheiddin Ellabbad, whose visual interpretation of the text enriched my work. The cover is enlivened by artist Adel El Siwi's inspired and evocative illustration. Without the moral support of my father, Youssef Halim, this translation would not have been possible: I therefore dedicate it to him.

An Old Fisherman

The waters of the lake flow languidly as they approach the sea. The lake's distant shore that blends into the horizon emerges swathed in mist and looms pale gray, revealing curvatures and protrusions, then it twists, mud-dark, in a sharp bend.

The reeds and brush thicken as the lake's two shores draw closer and proceed sinuously to form a narrow channel with thick mud seeping over its banks. The reeds disappear as the channel approaches the sea, where the sandy shore sprawls with its huge, dark rocks.

The waves of the lake chase each other lazily, small and even like the lines of a ploughed field. Drawn by the roar of the sea at the end of the channel, the waves flow toward it, now constricted by the two banks. The regular pattern they have long kept is disordered, and a violent movement churns beneath the tranquil surface. They rush, murky and turbid, weeds and algae bursting out from their depths, with a tinge of mud and a low rumble.

The waves of the sea invade the channel, their clamor resonating deep into it, and the tremulous waters of the lake succumb to them. The confluence yields a glimmer, spray, dark spume that floats along the muddy shore, and small bubbles that scatter agitatedly. Silvery fish, fins folded in, leap in an arch as if to cross the clamorous confluence, then plunge in again.

The place remained unfrequented for a long time. The sea was unknown to the fishermen of the lake, who had no experience of it. They stop with their small boats at the edge of the lake, sometimes holding onto the reeds at the sides of the channel, lashed by the tumultuous waves of the sea. They feel their boats being hurled about, crashing against the turbulent waters. The younger fishermen shout in exhilaration, as if undertaking their greatest adventure, but they do not keep it up for long, and soon they are rowing forcefully back into the open lake. These fishermen were born and raised on the lake's islands and found security in its tranquil waters. They cast their nets and stand at the tips of their boats, shouting to each other, or sometimes lie down inside, drinking tea and dozing, leaving the boats adrift. Finally, they alter the course of the boats with a few oar-strokes.

2

An old fisherman had come one day and settled in the area. They always saw him as old, perhaps because of the many wrinkles on his face and the stoop of his shoulders. It was said that he had no kin, for he had never been seen with anyone. He wandered day and night in his boat on the lake, and when exhaustion overcame him and he yearned for the land, he would throw anchor in the nearest spot and fall asleep. Sometimes, they passed his boat adrift in the middle of the lake, and saw him lying inside. Though the boat had two powerful oars, he rarely used them. Instead, he would pull them up onto the boat and unfurl his tattered sail with its many patches. He was unhurried, simply using the sail for shade when the sun was scorching. His boat was unlike the other boats on the lake, which were slender and pointed at both ends. His was wide and shell-shaped, its stern flat, with a pole at both ends and a rope in between on which he hung all his belongings. A net of gray thread that ended with large pieces of cork and a small anchor were on the prow. The fishermen of the lake did not use anchors, simply sticking a pole beside the boat to hamper its movement. Their nets were of white thread with round pieces of cork. His boat was coated to its edge with tar, giving off that black color which shimmers from afar in the sunlight, provoking gloom in those who see it. The fishermen on the lake and the inhabitants of the islands muttered their invocations whenever they caught sight of it and averted their eyes whenever it approached. But they seldom saw it, and long months could elapse before it returned to the same spot.

No one had seen a similar boat in any part of the wide lake. This is why they conjectured that he had come from other, distant regions. For some reason, they surmised that he was a fugitive: it might have been his grim demeanor as of one shouldering all the burdens of the world, his profound, piercing gazes, or his amazing capacity for stealth.

Totally unaware, they would suddenly find him passing an oar-stroke away from them. He would be lying in the bottom of the boat with his faded shawl on his face. They would sense his eyes peering at them between the folds of the shawl, and no sooner would they busy themselves with other things than they would see he had sailed far off.

One of them who had traveled to the capital to be treated for the bite of a rabid dog once said that he had seen similar boats on the Nile, and that the old fisherman must have slipped in one day through one of the rivulets that branch off the Nile and flow into the lake. They did not concern themselves with him for long, though. These were just a few words they spoke one day years ago, before they left him to his tireless, endless wanderings.

He would pass by the nearest village on the lake carrying a basket filled with whatever fish he had caught, which he then sold to the first bidder without bargaining, or gave to the grocer in return for whatever he needed—matches, gasoline, halvah, and tobacco. On his way back to the boat he would stop by the house with the open door to buy bread. But since they did not sell bread, they would just give him some loaves then fill him a small barrel with fresh water that he carried on his shoulder.

One day his boat entered the channel. He sat up from his prone position at the tremor of the boat and its swift streaming and saw the clamorous waves facing him. He rowed the boat close to the bank and threw the anchor. Settling quietly in the bottom of the boat, he looked around him with dazed, moist eyes. The waves of the sea curled and thinned out, their spray glistening in the sunlight. The waters of the lake churned at the confluence, their murmur lost amidst the roar of the waves. The opposite bank—curvatures and protrusions, covered with thick, green reeds—was a few oar-strokes away. And it was as if all these years he had been seeking to see the other shore. He contemplated it raptly. He made tea and drank it. He walked a long way on the shore of the lake, through the fallow, empty land, then returned. Later, he walked for a short while on the sandy seashore and gathered dry weeds. At night, he lit a fire and lay down in the boat.

In the morning, he drew a line tracing out a rectangle a few steps from the bank of the channel. In the middle he planted a short stick and left.

He did not return for three years. When he came back, he was very emaciated and his shoulders were stooped. He found no sign of the line he had traced, but his stick was still there. After taking a wide tour of the area, he gathered weeds, lit a fire, had tea, and lay down in the boat. In the morning, he planted another stick then left.

This time, he was away for a year and a half before coming back. His step was slow and the sparkle in his eyes had faded. He threw down his load of tree branches beside the stick and left.

In his wanderings he would pick up whatever objects he happened upon, and when many of them had collected in the boat, he would head for one of the small, unfrequented islands and hide what he had gathered there.

Sometimes, he buried the objects on a shore far from habitation.

He now passed by his many caches, spread along the length of the lake, guided by a familiarity he sensed on approach. After loading his boat, he would head for the channel. He spent months coming and going, and a mound of objects accumulated on the bank of the channel: wooden planks and metal sheets of different sizes, pegs, rolls of wire, ropes, iron rods, slabs from palm tree trunks, bricks, bits of jute and reed mats, empty cans and bottles, and seven sacks of corn cobs, many of which were spoiled by long storage.

Slowly the ragged hut rose: four supports from palm tree boards for which he had dug deep and three walls made of a mixture of wooden planks, reeds, and tree branches entwined with rope. The roof was of metal sheets. When they began shaking with the gusts of wind, he put some stones on top of them. He daubed the walls with mud mixed with bits of straw and built a wide brick bench inside. He was undecided about the door. In the end, he made a partition from tree branches and reeds and fixed it to the side with bits of rope for a hinge.

It was nighttime when he closed the door and lay down in the boat. He set out at dawn. The boat went forth swiftly to the far end of the lake, close by the mouth of a river. He spent the night fishing, drawing out his nets guided by the moonlight. In the morning his boat came ashore at a village he had been to twice before. On both occasions, he had given the fish to a woman who had offered him a seat on a stone beside her in the market. While selling the fish, she gave him a loaf of soft bread and an onion, and ordered tea for him from the café across from them.

3

The market was always crowded at that time of day. Men and women fishmongers sat under an awning made of reed sticks and jute. In front of them were basins and pots full of water they sprinkled from time to time over the fish. The fishermen came and gave their catch to the traders they knew.

He glimpsed her in her place amid the crowd, in her black gallabiya and veil and her brown drawers with the green dots and wide seat, covering her outstretched leg halfway. The basin in front of her was empty and a pitcher full of water was beside it. She was taking bites from a loaf on her lap. When she saw him, her eyes lingered over his face, as if trying to remember him, then she caught a glimpse of the two baskets and the customers who were following him. They had tried to stop him before he entered the market to see the fish he had with him, but when he paid no attention to them, they followed him. Her face lit up when she saw him heading toward her. Getting up to help him take down the two baskets from his shoulders, she said, "Haven't seen you in a long time."

He set down his fine, abundant catch of mullet, eel, and Nile perch on the stone beside her. She did not have the time to settle with him on a price. The customers surrounded her as she stood emptying the fish into the basin. She said to him, "Here's the bread," and pointed to a parcel beside him, "and there's the tea," and pointed to the café.

The selling did not take long. She filled several trays with fish, decorated each of them with an eel, and let the customers inspect them. When one of the trays emptied, she refilled it from the basin. She had finished and was gathering the money from her lap when he spoke to her of going away with him.

She looked at him hesitantly. His head was bowed and he was scratching the ground with a piece of straw. She folded in her outstretched legs, covered them with the gallabiya, and looked around her for the pitcher of water. Every now and then she rubbed her teeth with snuff to alleviate the ache, which left a dark mark on them. A smell of rotten weeds emanated from her mouth. He raised his head when he heard the sound of her gargling with water. She spat to the side and said, "I have two sons."

"Bring them along."

She eyed him silently. His face was parched like the bark of a tree. "And the boat?" she asked.

"With me."

That was not what she had meant. She had wanted to say that he and his black boat frighten her. She said, "Where?"

"There," he gestured with his hand.

"There, where?" she asked.

"At the channel."

"You went far."

"Not far."

"There's no one there."

"They'll come."

"And the house?"

"You'll see it."

She started counting and sorting the money she had collected. She was no longer young, but neither was she as old as he: the hair hidden under her veil was still black and shiny. Thinking of what her hair felt like when she braided it, she smiled. She gathered the empty trays inside the basin and felt the area around her. "And you?" she asked.

He gazed at her without speaking. She asked again, "And your children?" His eyes blinked for an instant. He said, "I'll be waiting for you in the boat."

She watched him as he walked away avoiding the crush of the market. He walked with a stoop; she said to herself it was from the long hours of bending over the oars. He trod with feet wide apart; she thought it was seldom that his feet touched firm ground. She smiled. "Some say he's a murderer, and some say he's a doomed man. Murderer or doomed man, why should I be afraid of him?"

He dragged the boat onto the shore and labored over it, cleaning it. He stuffed all his odds and ends into the hold in the fore and closed its hatch. He took out the old, moldy bedding, dried the bottom of the boat and left it to sun for a while. He spread fresh reeds and pushed the boat into the water, then sat on a rock beside it.

When the sun was about to set, he saw her coming, carrying on her head the basin, from which jutted a mat and a quilt rolled and tied with a rope. The two boys were behind her, one carrying a basket, the other a laden sack. She was in the same black gallabiya but instead of the veil she had tied a yellow scarf around her head. She sat facing him, the boys behind her sneaking glances at him over her shoulders. They were about ten years old and hard to distinguish from each other: the same features, hair color, eyes, and height. When she noticed him staring at them she laughed and said they were twins, one an hour older than the other. When she found that people couldn't tell them apart, she put a ring in the ear of the older one, but that same day the boys disappeared and came back in the evening giggling. The other one had a ring in his ear.

"Yes. He watched me pierce his brother's ear. He stole the needle and they did it. I said, 'I leave it to God. Their features will change when they grow up.'"

He looked at the small metal ring in the right ear of each boy as they leaned over the sides of the boat to touch the water. She said that their father had died years before. He rowed silently until the boat emerged into the open lake, then he pulled up the oars and unfurled the sail.

4

From his place in the boat where he is fixing the fishing net, he sees the smoke rising from the stove behind the hut in successive waves that the wind disperses. The woman comes and goes, and his eyes follow her until she is out of sight. His fingers run with the thread between the holes of the net. The three chickens, which she brought with their feet tied, peck at the ground. The boys rummage through the odds and ends he brought from his caches. A scrawny dog, which turned up suddenly after they settled in, follows the boys wherever they go, wagging its tail and barking mildly. One day he sees the boys bring out from among the odds and ends the iron rods and empty wooden thread spools, and remembers that he has collected many of them. The boys put the rods through the hollows of the spools and extend above them wooden planks they affix with a thin wire. In minutes they have made two carts they pull with ropes and load with what pieces of brick they find. They run off with the carts then return panting. They park the carts in front of the door of the hut and unload the bricks to load the small, empty barrels of water, and then dash off again, with the dog close at their heels. After a long absence, they return moist with perspiration and dust. Their mother comes out of the hut at the sound of their shouts. The barrels are full. They say they have found a stream of water by the trees, but when he looks in the direction they are pointing to, he sees no trees. After moving the barrels inside, they turn and look at him. Their mother says, "I left the water jug there. If you could fetch it for me."

The boys rarely approach him. When they pass beside his boat where he is seated, they fall silent until they have moved away. He brings them sugarcoated almonds and caramel on his return from one of his trips. He sees them standing at a distance while their mother empties the boat. When he stretches his hand out to her with the two paper cones filled with sweets, they take one step forward, but remain in their place until their mother comes back to them. Then they follow her into the hut. Shortly afterwards, they rush out, each holding a cone. They look at him deliberately then steal behind the hut.

The boys disappear at suppertime. The fire in front of the hut lights the area all the way to the shore. As she calls them, the woman sets the pot of rice and the vessel of fish by the fire. Then she walks a little way until the darkness engulfs her and her call rings out. He gets out of his boat, goes to the hut, and sits in front of the pot and the vessel. She sits beside him, not eating, waiting for the boys to return. She chatters, picks out the big fish, puts them in front of him, and peels onions for him. He takes the glass of tea from her and relaxes for a bit, struggling with sleep, gazing toward the prow of the boat, which the light has overtaken. She throws cobs and bits of wood into the fire and stares into the darkness.

Finally, he gets up and heads toward the boat. He sees the boys when they return. They sit beside their mother and after supper stretch out, each cushioning himself on one of her legs. She carries them one after the other into the hut, and he sees the fire die out, the embers still glowing for a while.

He goes back to his wanderings on the lake, staying away for a day or two and spending as long at the channel. The woman watches him walking along the seashore until he is out of her sight. Later she sees him moving around slowly inside the boat, shaking out the bedding and covers. He sits tense and gloomy, wrapped in an old gallabiya, staring at the water. At moments like this, he appears to have aged all of a sudden. He is emaciated, and his face is gaunt. She is afraid to approach him. He suddenly turns to her, his eyes bloodshot as if he has not slept all night. She thinks, now he will sail, and then she sees him sail.

Sometimes, he returns at night. The boat moors soundlessly in the channel. The lamplight sifts like splinters from the sides of the hut. The smell of the food she has cast aside for the chickens rises, and the embers glow with the gusts of wind. The dog crouching beside her does not move at his arrival. She goes to him at dawn and stands at his head, her hand on the prow. She leans forward to see him, and as if he has sensed her presence, she finds his eyes, as always, gazing at her. He is usually exhausted, huddled in the cover. She empties the boat's load for him. Things she has asked for and things he has brought of his own accord are piled up in the stern. She asks him about the spot where he fished, the kind of fish, the village where he sold them, and the price they paid. He answers in a murmur, as if overcome by sleep. He will have selected some fish and brought them back. She turns them over, then goes back to the hut as a murky light appears on the horizon.

One day he brought her a big mirror as tall as she was. She carried it to the hut, running together with the two boys. She stood in front of it with the boys at her sides. For the first time, they saw themselves from head to toe.

After that, the two boys would be in front of the hut eating and suddenly say, "The mirror," and carry the pot of food inside. They would sit in front of it, their hands scooping from the pot and rising slowly to their mouths. Undressing, they would stand side by side and gaze at their reflections. She, too, got into the habit of sitting cross-legged in front of the mirror every day, combing her hair. Contemplating her face and the two braids on her bust, she would throw one then the other on her back. In the end she would undo them both and gather up her hair under the black scarf.

He brought three chairs, each with two armrests and leather upholstery. The leather was cracked, the stuffing spilling from tears in the sides, but they were sturdy chairs. He put them inside the hut beside the mirror. On those nights when the old man was away the boys would bring out the chairs and set them on the shore and sit on them in the nude with their mother, each with his legs crossed, sucking on the sugar cane stalks he brought them.

He also brought two mattresses toward the beginning of winter, and iron sheets with which he lined the sides of the hut, so that the warmth spread inside at night.

The smell of grilled fish would waft out at sunset. He would be lying down in the boat, seeing one side of her back when she bent over the stove. Her lean body had filled out in those few weeks and her face had become rosy. He would glimpse the boys astride two wooden planks, penetrating the clamorous sea waves. Their bodies glistened in the dusk light. They parted their legs and waved their arms to keep their balance. The waves yielded to them. They rose and fell. Sometimes the waves flung them, and they shrieked. He saw them as two distant spots. Then he saw them approach in the wink of an eye. Night was falling fast.

5

The preparation of the hut did not take long, since she had only brought a few things, which she threw here and there. The boys, who normally followed her wherever she went, left her to look at the sea, returned, then left her once again to search out the area behind the hut. It was late and pitch dark. She walked to the boat and saw him fast asleep. There would be time in the morning, she thought, and went back to the hut and slept with the boys clinging to her.

In the morning he had set out, but by sunset he returned again. She grilled the fish and they had supper in front of the hut. Sitting not far away, she watched him out of the corner of her eye. He was engulfed in silence, taking the glow of the fire into his palm with his arm stretched over his knee, absently looking at the sea. He drank tea then returned to the boat.

From where she was sitting, she watched the boat sway lightly, close to the shore. The fire was dying out with small tongues of flame suddenly darting out from among the glowing embers. The boys were asleep on her legs. She carried them inside, walked to the beach, shook the boat with her hand, and sat on a rock by the prow. She looked around and announced to him that the boys were asleep.

She undid her headscarf and threw the two braids onto her bust, rolled up the gallabiya to her waist, and waded through the waters of the lake. Heavy clouds screened off the moon, and the water was dark and warm. The small waves lashed her forcefully and the spray splashed on her face. The roar of the sea resonated deep into the channel and a fleeting shudder went through her. She cupped the water in her palms and washed her thighs, her belly, and under her breasts. On her way back to the shore, she leaned on the boat's edge, shook it slightly, and laughed. She stood on the rock holding the gallabiya rolled up from her body to dry. She heard him murmuring, as if talking to himself, that his best days were behind him and that pain tore at his innards. As she stood there, leaning slightly, she saw him lying in the bottom of the boat, and his head without the turban was small and bare. He lay on his side with his hand under his chin.

She said that the lake was merciless at night, that many suffer from the same ache that he had, and that she would put a pack of hot bran on it to ease the pain. Then she went to the hut and brought back the pack. His body felt small in her hands as she tightened the wrap around his waist and pulled the cover over him.

When winter came she told him to come and sleep in the hut. He said he was used to sleeping in the boat and brought out from the hold a lamb's wool cloak that he added to the cover and a brown shawl that he wrapped around his shoulders.

She got into the habit of going to him in the boat with the teakettle and then sitting on the rock in the bright sun. She would see his thin legs uncovered and stretched out to the warm rays, and his head propped against the edge of the boat. Now that she felt at ease with him, she told him her secret: her husband had not died.

Taking a sip of tea from the glass, she watched him out of

the corner of her eye. He was gazing at the two boys gliding among the sea waves on the wooden planks.

She smiled and added that he had not even been her husband.

She smiled once again before going on. She was seated behind his head watching the boys disappear behind the huge billows then reappear, spray scattering around them.

He had been a labor contractor who took her away one afternoon, after they had finished transplanting the rice seedlings into the basins. The girls had returned on the tractor to the village. She hid under the wooden bridge as he had instructed her, then took the train with him.

"He bought me a pair of slippers, two gallabiyas, a slip and a headscarf."

He had told her that his sister lived in the neighboring village.

She followed him after they got off the train. The village resembled her own, except that everything in it was different. It had the same long, winding street with shops on either side: a butcher, a grocer, a gallabiya-maker, and a shop that sold roasted seeds where he bought her a paper cone-full that she emptied into the pocket of her gallabiya. He brought his chest, which he kept at a café, and put what he had bought her in it. She carried the chest on her head.

They walked down a road outside the village with no sign of any vehicles on it. Night fell as they walked. Resting under a tree on the bank of a canal, they ate bread, halvah, and felafel from a parcel he had in the chest. Then he lay her on the bank of the canal. She began to cry and he told her to stop. She leapt screaming when the frogs hopped on her face, but he muffled her mouth with his hand, pushed her down, and entered her once again.

Later, she washed in the waters of the canal. When she finished, he told her he would have a short nap and that she should wake him up when she heard the evening call to prayer, and he fell asleep with his arm resting on the chest.

She was afraid of the dark, the void, and the blood seeping from her. She washed again then lay down beside the chest and slept. She woke at his kick. It was dawn and he was angry. He brought out her new clothes from the chest, took away her old ones and threw them in a nearby cornfield. She carried the chest and walked behind him.

"He told his sister that he was taking me to Hajj Umran's house in town, where I would be working."

Waiting at the door of the house, she saw a child crawling in front of the threshold with sticky dust around its mouth. She heard him call her from within.

"His sister is a hawk. She looked me up and down, her eyes fixed on my breasts."

Her breasts are large. Ever since she became aware of them at the age of thirteen, she made a point of walking with her shoulders drawn back, to bring out their curves. She could see them swinging as she walked, and whenever she was alone, she would feel them with pleasure. She noticed men's eyes on her breasts. They would stop her and say anything that came into their heads.

"Whose daughter are you, girl?"

"Who do you work for, girl?"

She would just laugh, toss back her two braids, and walk away. Her mother sewed a bra for her from an old gallabiya, but when she put it on she felt that it suffocated her, even though it did not stop her breasts from shaking. On her way back from the mill the boys would leave the other girls and walk near her. Two or three boys awaited the girls on their way back on the empty path by the canal, hiding in the dark behind an extinguished brick kiln. They said things that made her angry, then put out their hands to touch her breasts and ran away. She would scold and swear at them. They followed her with their gallabiyas rolled up and tied around their waists, their eyes glimmering in the dark. She would hear the sound of their panting as one after the other jumped in front of her. She was not afraid of them and avoided their outstretched hands. Sometimes one of the hands reached her breast and squeezed it, and she screamed. They would keep up their chase of the girls until they reached the first of the village houses.

"We had lunch and dinner at her place."

She ate alone in the courtyard, listening to them eating and chattering in the lit room.

"I swept the house for her, did the laundry, and washed up."

The sister's eldest son followed her with his eyes. His neck was long and scrawny, his face the color of a lemon. He sat cross-legged on the sofa, studying under the lamp. The bed, which had black posters, was in the back of the room. The other sons sat studying around a low table in the space in front of the bed. Their mother—the man's sister—lay on the mat, legs spread, the child in her lap. She sat at the woman's feet mending her sons' torn gallabiyas. The sister asked her about her people, her village, and what the brother did there.

"My tongue must have slipped."

She sensed it when she saw the sister suddenly fall silent. She had prepared her bedding to sleep in the courtyard as the sister had told her, but as she was getting up to go, the sister said for her to fetch her bedding and sleep with them in the room. Her husband and her brother slept in another room. The sister, the two boys and the child got into the bed and she told her eldest son who was going to sleep on the sofa to extinguish the lamp when he had finished studying. The sister stretched out by the wall opposite the sofa and pulled the cover over her face.

She sensed the boy when he came and slipped in beside her under the cover. She had her ear to the bed where the sister lay with her back turned to the room, her breathing heavy and loud. She became aware—before she abandoned herself to the boy—of the sound having stopped, as if the sister was listening to them.

They left in the morning. His sister walked them to the door, patted her on the back as she was leaving and placed a parcel of food in her hand.

The chest was heavier than before. He had gathered in it all his clothes that were at his sister's. They took the train, and then walked once again on the road. "All roads look alike."

He said they were going to one of his other sisters—

there were four—so he could fetch some of the things he had left with her. He was walking slowly, striking the hem of his gallabiya with a cane and watching the sun set. They left the road for a sidetrack. He was heading for an abandoned water-wheel she saw after they had passed through the corn fields. They sat on a hay stack beside it, and he unwrapped the parcel of food: a roasted chicken and rice. He gave her a chicken leg. She hesitated to take it; never in her life had she had a whole leg to herself. Her mother slaughtered a chicken when it fell sick and no one would buy it, and her share would be part of the leg. He also gave her the neck and the head—always her mother's share.

The grains of rice stuck to his thick mustache. It was getting dark and he was staring at her with murky eyes, his mouth drooping. Sometimes as she sat she would sense him looking at her and would turn and see his murky eyes, the color of dust, his salivating mouth and heavy, panting breathing, and would know that he wanted her and that she was to set aside whatever she was doing, wash her face and go to him before he kicked her. She lay on her side on the hay and waited for him.

Later, she followed him to wash in a stream on the other side of the water-wheel. The water was cool. She lay on her back and let her body be submerged while her hands clung to the bottom.

When she returned, she found him asleep with his arm on the chest. The hay was damp, and the darkness deep from afar. She gazed into it and shuddered. At the evening call to prayer, she woke him up and they set out.

*

The old man moves in the boat, turning in his prone position, and mutters a few words to which she does not pay attention. With half-closed eyes, he watches the two boys who have collided and fallen amidst the waves. The two wooden planks are afloat, bobbing about, the boys nowhere to be seen. Then they loom far off, the spume scattering around them.

She watches him out of the corner of her eye. Sitting on the rock, leaning forward with her elbows on her knees, she is looking in the same direction he is. Then she catches a glimpse of the boys. She says that she has been looking at them all the time but not really seeing them, then becomes more alert. She is careful not to recount everything to him. Her voice rises from time to time to reach him in the boat, then falls to a whisper. Her big toe scratches the sticky shore. Finally, she falls silent, her eyes on the rippling waters of the channel. Never before has she harked back to what has passed. It is as if she had been running breathlessly all along. And she would never have looked back had it not been for this old man who suddenly sprouted from nowhere, who is now lying in the boat, whose face she cannot even see. She says, "His four sisters. And his relatives. A day here, a day there."

He gathered his belongings from their houses until the chest was full to the brim. His paternal cousin, a government employee, wore pajamas and left his head uncovered, as if pleased with his black hair glistening with oil.

Without raising his eyes he stole a glance at her breasts, while she was bending, pouring water for his ablutions, dressed in his wife's cotton flannel gallabiya. It was tight and threadbare at the chest, showing her calico slip heavy with her breasts. He asked her if she had served in houses before.

"No."

"The first time?"

She said it was the first time, and he motioned with his head to the room where his cousin sat.

"And him?"

"What about him?"

"Is he taking you somewhere?"

"Yes. He's escorting me somewhere."

Shaking the water off his hand, he touched her breast, as if by accident. "I don't like this sort of person. He does something and pretends he's not doing it."

The cousin's house was big and clean. It had everything in it: sacks of rice and wheat arranged in a room, together with jars of ghee and cheese, and on the roof was a chicken and duck coop, as well as a pigeon house. He told her to go up to the roof.

She was sweeping the courtyard, his wife's voice overheard chatting with a woman neighbor in the alley. He stood clinging to her from behind. She moved away then turned to him, bewildered. Looking around him, he whispered, "Go up to the roof," and she went.

The parapet around the roof was a meter high. There were bundles of hay and dry firewood, and the washing was on the lines. She stretched out her legs and looked at the chickens crouched quietly in the coop behind the wire-screen. When he emerged from the top of the staircase, he hurried toward her, bending to hide beneath the parapet. He dropped to his knees beside her and stretched out his hand to her breast. She felt his other hand running under her gallabiya. He was panting. Then he left her and rushed downstairs.

The sun was bright; it hurt her eyes. She shook out the bits of straw clinging to her hair and gallabiya. The clothes on the line had dried and were fluttering lightly in the breeze.

They were walking on the road. The labor contractor told her that his cousin whom she had seen was dirty. Then he gave her a long look. The chest on her head was heavy and sweat was streaming down her face. They sat under a mulberry tree, the canal beside them tiled and clear. Water rushed from a pipe with a wide mouth, and she threw herself naked underneath it, cupping the water in her hands and laughing. When he gestured to her to come out, she just went on laughing. The gusts of water on her head made her dizzy, so she threw herself away from the mouth of the pipe for a moment then went back to it. Sometimes he was kind and did not beat her. At such moments he appeared to have drifted far. His arm outstretched over his knee, he settled for pulling her to his side.

She was wrapped in the gallabiya she had taken off. He placed the chest between his legs. The padlock hanging from the staple was large. He gave her the soiled clothes, his and hers, and a bar of soap. He was rummaging in the chest when she went to the canal. She washed the clothes and hung them on the tree branches. The soap smelled good. She went back to the stream and washed. Then he took out a new change of clothing for her and she put it on. The slip was as soft as silk. With the new gallabiya still in his hand, he looked at her. Her shoulders and half her bosom were bare beneath the slip's two thin straps. He gestured for her to approach. The gallabiya was yellow with a green print in the form of willow leaves.

At times he seemed to be jesting with her. He would smile slightly with the corner of his mouth, his eyes on her, as if suppressing a secret. She would drop her guard, feeling him close to her, and say to herself that he was like her, stricken by life; then she would laugh, unfurl her hair and prance about. He brought out from the chest a blue necklace, which he dangled from the tip of his finger, and three bracelets of the same color, which he held in the fingers of his other hand. She laughed, spun around herself, and swayed on the tips of her feet, drawing closer to him.

The boat rocks violently and collides with the shore. She sees the old man suddenly sit up and turn to her. He appears to have woken up from a slumber. The two boys in the midst of the waves are farther apart. He coughs and lies down again. The wave retreats and the boat settles to a light sway.

She says he wasn't their father.

She readies to get up, then sits back and stretches out her legs. His eyes are fastened on the two boys in the sea.

She says the labor contractor lodged her in that house that he saw in the village. It was a room with a courtyard. He had said he had bought it for her, and later she came to know he was renting it. He had told people that she was his wife.

"Who would doubt his words?"

He dressed in a woolen gallabiya and wrapped a silk shawl on his shoulders over the cashmere overcoat. He was clean-shaven and his plump cheeks were always rubbed with cologne. He sat with men from the neighborhood at the cafés.

"They'd believe him. I don't know what he said to them, but why shouldn't they believe him?"

He came once a week, sometimes twice. There was no fixed routine. He would spend a night or two with her then go. He usually brought a reed parcel containing meat parts and trotters. Fatigued, he undressed without looking at her or talking to her. She caught the clothes he threw and hung them on nails in the wall where he had pasted newspaper sheets. Then he lay down in his underwear on the bed—a wide brick bench along the wall. Once every two weeks she changed the straw on it. The straw was covered with a woolen cloak, over which she spread a sheet. When she woke him up to have dinner, he would be recovered and look about. She would tell him what she had done during his absence, including what she bought from the shop, so that he could settle the account. He would open the chest and bring out her red satin nightgown and his light gallabiya, two bottles of cologne—one for him and one for her—her blue velvet slippers with the red flowers and the small towels she used. These he himself put under the pillow.

He said to her he was tired of life, that people have no mercy. He said it every time he came. She did not utter a word at his side. He took her on his arm and said that since he was very young he had not stopped wandering from village to village and from farm to farm, that his work, which many envied, exhausted him, that his legs no longer supported him.

A dim light filtered in through the door that gave onto the courtyard, and her eyes settled on it. The sound of heavy breathing rose from his open mouth.

He would wake her up at dawn, and she would see him bathing in the basin at the threshold of the courtyard, his body huge, his back turned to her. He said the toilet was narrow and that he was afraid of the geckoes nesting there. He was bad tempered when he got up. Waiting for daybreak, he would have breakfast, get dressed, and drink tea. She would sit silently on the mat, her back propped against the brick bench, not daring to go back to bed for more sleep.

When she told him she was pregnant, he hit her. She had thought he was the father. He suddenly turned around and smacked her. "You too!" he shouted. Terrified by his anger, she crawled out of reach of his hands. He followed her, his face overcast and contorted, spittle scattering from his mouth. He said that this was what he expected. All along he was waiting, saying to himself she might be different from the others, saying she must be different from the others, that the likes of her want marriage and a home, and because he is sterile, he has to wait: it is written that he should wait and watch. And every time he leaves the house and the village . . . Ah! And why shouldn't he have protected them too from scandal! Even his four wives—all of them. Each one of them says, "Your son." The slut. My son.

He beat her violently with both hands. She huddled in a corner, her nose bleeding, a terrible heaviness in her eyes, which began to swell. He kicked her, aiming for her belly but she bent over and it caught her in the shoulder. She moved away from his feet. While he was casting around for something to hit her with, she rushed out into the courtyard. She screamed and ran. He followed her, hurling at her whatever he found. He bent down, panting, and swore at her. Standing at the outer wall, she prepared to climb it. He stayed bent, watching her, then returned to the room. She could see him inside, gathering his belongings. He folded the blanket he brought the time before last, and the woolen cloak on the brick bench after he had shaken off the clinging straw. She stood a few steps away from the door to the courtyard. He opened the chest and threw in whatever his hands fell on. The satin nightgown. The glass in which he drank his tea. The new veil he bought her and the blue velvet slippers. His underwear pinned on the line. She ran away when he went into the courtyard to gather it. It was still damp.

He closed the chest, put it on his shoulder, and with the blanket and cloak under his arm, he left.

*

She looked at the old man and listened attentively. He was lying on his back, propped on his arm.

In the sea the two boys were riding the wooden planks once more, hand in hand, swaying on the waves.

She got up, went into the hut and came back carrying a pillow, which she placed under the old man's head.

He told her that the boys had gone far and gestured toward the sea. A tremulous look was in his eyes, and a grayish hue had crept on the sides of his face. He looked at her as if wanting her to say something. She said they would return and asked him if he would like to sit by the fire near the hut. He said he was comfortable in the boat.

As she sat on the rock, the lake water rose until it flooded the shore and wetted her feet. The sea waves were rushing into the channel. Squeezed out by the banks, their spindrift scattered high.

She said that he had carried the chest and left.

"The house is far out—you saw it. Outside the village. You hear their voices at daybreak when they return from the lake. You don't hear them afterwards."

She would stand at the end of the courtyard atop an old upturned barrel, leaning with her arms on the edge of the high wall, looking from afar at the lake. The shimmer of the light on the water's surface faded with the fading of the day. There was an expanse of cultivated fields and beyond them stretched vast areas of arid land where balls of dry brambles rolled, finally pushed by the wind into the lake where they floated for a while then disappeared into the water.

At night a deep stillness reigned, interrupted by the croaking of many frogs, and when they fell silent she could make out the murmur of the lake water as it lapped the shore.

"So scared was I that I used to leave the door ajar. I'd close the door to the courtyard and leave the door to the street ajar. The street doesn't frighten me as much as the lake. I walked along its shore once or twice. What I don't know scares me."

She started to consider closing the street door too, having heard the barking of the dogs and their fights, which sometimes reached into the room. It was then that they came. When they found the door ajar, they entered. They were strangers. She had not seen them in the village, and even if she had seen them she would not have recognized them. They used to come from the lake. She would be asleep and wake up at the low grating of the door.

They came to spend the evening at the cafés of the village. They had no fixed schedule. They dragged their boats onto the shore, passing by the house on their way to the village. It became their habit that one of them would stay behind and the others would go on. Sitting in bed, she would see him place the basket full of fish behind the door, which he closed, extinguish the lamp, open the door to the dimly-lit courtyard, and take the shawl off his head.

The men moved about the house with familiarity, knowing where everything was. Once, one of them asked her to make a fire of cobs for the water-pipe. When she said she had none, he looked at her in astonishment, then got up. Bringing out the cobs from under the heap of logs in the corner of the courtyard, he said, "So the rain won't spoil them."

Another time when she said that she could not reach up the high wall, he said, "And the barrel?"

"What barrel?"

He jumped from her side and drew her to the courtyard. Pushing away part of the heap of logs, he brought out a barrel. He rolled it to the corner of the wall and raised her on it.

He said it had been Aunt Sekina's house.

He was standing in front of the stove in the courtyard, lighting the cobs. She was in bed watching his shadow extend in the moonlight to the front of the doorway. A sense of ecstasy suffused her as the shadow swayed right and left, and she laughed inwardly.

He said that for many years they used to come to see Aunt Sekina when they were boys. She was a kind old woman who always kept molasses candy bars for them in a cloth sack hung on a nail in the wall within their reach. She knew each and every one of their grandfathers. She would describe them, recount their ways and the kind of food they liked. With every telling, she would add something new they had not heard before. They listened to her with fascination. Some of them had not seen their grandfathers. Aunt Sekina always spoke of a grandfather they did not know and had never heard of, and when they asked their fathers about him no one remembered him. She said he hid at her place for two days. His wounds were many. In his head alone there were two long, knuckle-deep wounds. They had chased him in the village. Her aged face would light up when she recounted how he shoved them away when the fight broke out in the café. They tore his clothes. He was leaning against the wall returning their blows, covered in blood. They pulled him by his clothes to tear him away from the wall, and his long pants fell off. When they saw he was uncircumcised they were horrified.

"Savage."

They crowded around him and wanted to take him on a mock parade, with jeering and bawdy songs, but he shot out from their midst half naked, the blows raining down on him. He avoided houses and people and hid in a corn field. They surrounded it, calling to him to come out; it was pitch-dark and they could never have spotted him there. They stood around hesitantly, afraid of penetrating into the field without knowing where he was. While they were standing at the edges, waiting for the approaching dawn, he slipped out from the distant end of the field and moved from one field to another until he was far away. They discovered his escape with the light of dawn and rushed to the shore of the lake. When they found his boat they broke it and waited for him there.

Aunt Sekina was sitting on the threshold of the house, picking out the stones from a tray of rice in front of her. They passed by her and she returned their greetings. The wound in his head bled. She waited until night fell, shut him in, and went out. She brought the barber, who followed her from afar, hidden by the darkness. He stitched up the wound, while she put the lamp on her head and helped by pressing the two sides of the wound until they came together, and the barber drew the thread. The barber wrapped his head in gauze and said the dressing should be changed every day. The barber was sitting on the edge of the bed, sipping his tea, puffed up like a gander that had just come out of the canal. He said he had heard about the fight in the café, then fell silent, waiting. The grandfather covered himself with a sheet he wrapped around his waist. The barber stole glances at the lap of the grandfather, who was sitting cross-legged. Handing her the empty glass of tea, the barber said, "If necessary, I could circumcise you."

The grandfather acted as if no one was talking to him. Sipping the chicken soup from a bowl in his hand, his movements fell still for a moment. He handed her the empty bowl, burped loudly then turned around and contemplated the barber. Then he lay back and drew the cover over his face. The barber looked at her, then at him, put his hands in the pockets of his coat and left.

Aunt Sekina stole a pair of long pants from the washing that hung in front of a house and mended the tear in his gallabiya. When she brought him the pants, he put them on and got up. She told him he should wait for someone to come from the lake and return with him. He was reeling, his eyes turbid with fever. He pushed her aside and left.

She told herself that the night would hide him.

She followed him. He turned and said to her, "Go back."

And she went back.

By the lake, they were not expecting him. Those who had remained on the shore, three or four, did not bar his way. He threw himself into the lake. They saw him swim and disappear into the dark water and for a while they continued to hear the beating of his arms.

Aunt Sekina would fall silent. Sometimes, she would content herself with what she had said, or she would whisper, "Not even ten of them could've got the better of him."

Once when the boys insisted she tell them what had happened to him, she said that he had not made it, and when they asked how she knew, she said, "He would have come back to see me."

When she fell ill, their fathers came to take her to the lake. But she said she wanted to die in her own home. Her illness worsened, so they carried her to the boat. She was like a little girl on their shoulders, wrapped in a blanket. When they laid her down in the boat, she regained her awareness.

"Take me back home."

They stood around for a moment, not knowing what to do, then carried her back to the house. They put her in bed, and she said the sweets were in the sack. Then she gestured to the sack and died.

"Yes. She died. Not once did any of them come and not talk about her."

She contemplated the young man's face in the dim light. She thought to herself that they resembled each other. The same features, the same height and girth. The voice differed, as did the talk.

On their way back from the café, one of them would cough when they approached the house. He got up from her side, careful not to wake her. Still awake, she sensed him leave, heard the grating of the door as he pulled it behind him, his step quickening to catch up with the others. A heavy silence enveloped the room and courtyard, and the mice scurried in the gray light. The men's voices receded on their way to the lake. She closed the door. They reminded her of the faces of boys she used to play with in the alleyways. She said to herself that the leftovers were still in the pot on the stove. The smell of the food would draw the cats and she would be woken by the clang of the pot as it fell to the floor, and from beneath the door she would see the shadow of the stray dog as it came and lay down on the other side of the doorstep.

He was different from the others: slim, stooped, his nose pointed. Had she not heard the men's voices when they walked past the house she would not have thought he was one of them.

He stood hesitantly in the doorway, then took off his slippers, walked in slowly and sat on the edge of the bed. He said that when they heard about his visit to her they sent a basket of fish with him, and pointed to the basket at the door. They had also cooked her a drake, he said, and pointed to a smaller basket beside it, where she saw a pot with a lid. He stared at her with wide eyes and, feeling his scrutiny, she got up to warm the drake and the rice, which was mixed with white beans and tomatoes.

"Only the people of the lake cook mixed rice. They never

cook plain rice." She asked him who had cooked it. As she stood in front of the stove, she sensed his eyes on her back. She does not like being watched or stared at; it bewilders her.

He said his mother had prepared it with Umm Salem. "Her son Salem often comes to the village."

He described Salem and although she did not recognize him from the description, she said she may have seen him.

The sharp-featured face frightened her. He was a man of his word. He sat there, feeling his sides. His face was emaciated, as of one diseased. They had dinner on the mat. He ate slowly, chewing at length on his food, then washed his hands three times in the courtyard, while she poured water for him. Gargling, he raised his face and looked at her.

He sat with his back against the brick bench, his arm stretched along his bent knee. Not knowing what he was after, she felt confused. He smiled as he watched her. She got up and went out into the courtyard to look for something, then went back in. Finally she sat nearby.

He said he rarely came to the village, then fell silent for a while. Turning over an upturned slipper, he said that for years he had not left the lake. She wanted to ask what prevented him but refrained; she felt wary.

He said that he kept himself occupied out there, always finding something to do. He looked around him, examining the room, then leaned forward slightly to look at the courtyard through the open door. He said he never joined them when as young boys they had come to see Aunt Sekina. As soon as they were allowed to take the boats, they rowed toward her.

He asked her if she needed anything, and she answered that she had all she needed.

His voice sounded weak; it seemed that the food was too heavy for him. He said nothing further and remained seated until they passed by and he joined them.

The two boys disappeared amid the waves. The planks bobbed without them. Later she saw them, each clutching his plank with an arm and beating the water with the other. They were far apart, then drew close together. The old man propped himself up slightly on his arm then lay back again.

She said she used to carry the basket of fish to the market and no sooner did she get there than the customers grabbed them—she had never seen fish like them. Where had they gone to catch them? "I don't know. They resembled the fish you bring."

When the customers asked her where she got the fish she laughed.

"Big fish. Fleshy. With clean guts."

She said that when the men saw the chest they asked her, "Is it his chest?"

"It is."

One of them carried it on his shoulder and walked around with it. "It's heavy," he said.

"Yes, it's heavy. It breaks my back when I move it to sweep."

He carried it out into the courtyard, which was flooded

in moonlight. He went all the way to the wall then returned. Putting it back in its place, he said, "It resembles him."

"Resembles whom?"

"It resembles its owner. Everyone has a likeness with his things."

The men told her they had seen him once in the village. They recognized him by the cashmere overcoat she said he always wears. They said that when he turns round, he turns his whole body. She said that that was him: he always has neck aches. When they asked what kept her with him, she fell silent. She herself did not know. He did not scare her— he beat her and she received the blows in silence. And when pain overcame her she would rush out into the court-yard. Later she would slip into the room while he was asleep. She felt relieved whenever he left, as if a load had been lifted from her. But his chest was always with her. What was this strange intimacy she felt toward the chest? She had never opened it, never seen what was inside. It was closed with hasp and staple and a huge padlock. One day she made a table-cloth for it from an old slip of hers the color of onion peel, embroidered its edges with green thread, and in the middle set circles of beads and sequins she had taken from her scarf. The day he took the chest and left, she cried, beat her face, slammed the doors, threw herself on the mat, and thought she was going to die. She kept saying that he knew her, knew her village and her people. Now, no one knew her.

She would stand on the barrel looking into the open

space. The sunbeams were reflected on the distant waters. The lake no longer frightened her. She would leave the door to the courtyard open. Her full belly was growing more round under the gallabiya. They felt it. One of them would place his ear on it and listen. She said it moved; he said he could hear it.

The men did not stay for long in the house any more though. They talked to her while standing, looked at her belly and smiled, joked with her and sometimes did not even go in. They would stop on their way, knock on the door and leave the basket of fish.

They brought her soap, sugar, tea, a jar of ghee and half a bolt of cloth from which she eventually made five gallabiyas for each boy, apart from the diapers.

"Our son," they said.

The midwife came a week before delivery to stay with her. "Your relatives sent me," she explained.

When the midwife asked her about her term, she answered that she did not know, so the midwife felt her belly and said, "A week or two. Not more."

The midwife had her stay in bed. She washed, swept, cooked, and took the fish to the market. The men now passed by every day and left slaughtered chickens, fish, eggs, and jugs of milk. The day she gave birth the midwife said, "Your relatives are outside."

It was dusk. With a great effort, she went to the door. The pangs had started in the afternoon. The midwife must have known a day or two before she was due and let them know. She stood in the doorway looking at them.

Perspiration covered her and things reeled in front of her eyes. She saw them sitting by the track on the bank of a nearby dry canal. Anyone seeing them would have thought they were taking a short rest in the shade of the trees. Leaning against the door, a tremor coursing through her legs, she gazed at each of them and smiled. She remembered the features of four of them; the others had familiar faces.

The midwife went to them with the teakettle, the glasses, the water-pipe, and the plate of hot coals. The light of the kerosene lamp was weak, casting many shadows that danced in the room. When they brought the mantle-lamp, the midwife put out the kerosene lamp.

She asked the midwife if they were still outside.

"They're there."

"The bread is in the crate hanging on the wall in the courtyard, and the cheese and honey are in the box," she said to the midwife.

"They don't want anything," the midwife answered.

She screamed and caught her breath, panting. She sensed someone standing outside the door, the midwife whispering to him then pushing the door shut.

It was late when she gave birth, and they were still outside.

They kept coming from day to day. One of them would stand by the door and call out. She would ask him in, and he would put what he was carrying aside, pet the two boys a little and go. Then they suddenly stopped coming.

"I don't know where they went."

*

The sun finally disappeared, the dusk light glimmered far over the sea waves and a mild chill was in the air. She pulled her legs together and tucked the gallabiya around them. The boys were on their way back. Each straddled a wooden plank and, with his legs dangling to the sides, paddled with his arms. The clamor of the waves intensified and the waters of the lake grew troubled. The fire in front of the hut went out, no longer giving off smoke. The dog roamed around the door of the hut, and she shooed it away. She leaned against the side of the boat, as was her habit when she wanted to get up, and with the movement of the boat, she saw the old man turn over and fall face down.

6

The two boys were digging not far from the shore, waist-deep in the hole, taking turns with the blade of an axe they had found among the old man's odds and ends that were packed in two sacks behind the hut. They shoveled the sticky earth and threw it on either side. The corpse, covered in an old threadbare sheet, lay on wooden boards by the shore where they had washed it. The woman scooped up lake water in a pot, while the boys scrubbed the body with loofah and soap. She pointed to the armpits, the nostrils, and the ears. The boys spread out his arms and, squatting on their heels, moved around him. His body was small, with protruding bones. When they failed to turn him over to wash his back, the woman helped them push him on his side. She held onto his shoulders until they had finished. Then they left him for a short while to dry before covering him with the sheet.

The woman lit a big fire in front of the hut, dispelling the gloom around it. She fed the fire with many bits of wood. The light from the fire showed the boat rocking with the clashing waves of the channel. She towed the boat with the boys pushing it from the rear until it settled on the shore.

The boys sat on the sides of the hole, their legs dangling in it. The woman walked over to them. She said it was too small, and moved away. The boys jumped into the hole and went on digging.

They had their supper by the fire. The woman brought the pot of rice with the roasted fish on its lid from the stove, and they ate in silence while the dog lay quietly nearby. Afterwards, the boys went back to the hole and the woman remained by the fire, drinking tea.

She washed the pot in the channel and stood on the shore looking toward the sea. Her hair was loose, the wind blowing strong, the darkness hiding the roaring waves of the sea. She stood there for a long while, then turned back. She brought the old man's arms to his sides—the boys had left them spread out—and tucked the sheet around him.

She got into the boat and brought out all its contents: the blankets, the pillow, the moldy reed bedding. She found a chest in the hold of the boat. She and the boys carried it between them to the hut. It resembled the labor contractor's chest. Medium in size like it, the chest had the same jutting edge of the lid and was also dark green. The padlock hanging from the staple was covered with rust. They looked for the key in the pocket of the gallabiya they had taken off the old man, in the two pockets of the waistcoat, and in the boat.

Finally the boys broke the padlock open with the axe blade.

They sat around the chest, the lamp hanging from the wall above their heads. The woman brought out a blue woolen gallabiya, moth-eaten on the chest and shoulders, and a waistcoat, whose fabric retained its sheen. From its buttonhole the old man had hung a chain, which ended with a watch tucked into the pocket. She opened its metal lid, and placed her ear on it, but heard no sound. She handed it to the boys, who were leaning on her thighs watching her. Each in turn put it against his ear, then returned it to her. She took out a pair of black shoes into which he had inserted rags, a set of underwear—a pair of long underpants and a long-sleeved undershirt—and a wallet full of papers. She spread the papers on her lap. Inscribed in an indelible pencil, they were tattered. The lines that had been dampened had gone purple. The papers had been stamped at the bottom with small and big seals and carried finger-prints. In the bottom of the chest she found, wrapped in a piece of paper, prayer beads, of which two were missing, and a silver ring with a black stone.

She looked at the empty chest, with its inner sides lined with paper and a small hole in the corner where powdered wood was scattered. Each of the boys on her sides had put on a shoe. "All those years," she whispered.

She turned to the boys. "Put them back in the chest."

"And the watch?"

"And the watch."

The boys started arranging the things in the chest.

"He was keeping them for his return," she said.

"Where?"

"God knows."

"And what stopped him?"

"Only God knows. Maybe the time hadn't come."

"What time?"

"There's a time for all things."

They closed the chest. She hung the broken padlock from the staple and they carried the chest to the side of the hole. They dragged the corpse on the wooden boards. The boys went down into the hole, received the corpse, placed the chest beside it, and covered it with earth. Then they leveled the grave with their feet. Hand in hand they jumped on the grave with the darkness surrounding them, their mother sitting by the fire.

7

The gypsies come and go. They pitch tents not far from the lake, encouraged by the presence of the hut, the woman, and the two boys. Their skinny goats graze the weeds on the shore and follow the boys on their daily walk to the waterway, which widens day after day on its way to the lake. There are some workers digging, and as far as the eye can see there are tree tops, and land divided into basins inundated with water and rice seedlings, whose tips sway in the wind.

The gypsies spend days there, then take down their ragged tents and leave.

The boats come into the channel—three or four, sometimes five—guided by the dim light on the shore. Their owners grill fish and eat in a circle around the fire. Close to the glow, the two boys fall asleep after eating, cushioned on their mother's legs.

One night the boats sailed away, trailing the black boat with the woman and the two boys, and disappeared into the darkness of the vast lake.

In winter the winds buffeted the hut, blowing the iron sheets far off. Its posts—the four palm tree planks—continued to resist stubbornly. He had dug deep to secure them.

Sea Gale

8

Urbanization has crept north toward the lake. Small one-story houses have been hastily built with concrete. They have wide brick benches, narrow courtyards, and flat roofs, many of which remain incomplete. Bits of rope and tatters, flung by the wind, cling to the rusty iron rods that jut out of them. Shops occupy the corners of houses, or sometimes a wall with a window, and are marked out by barrels of oil and gasoline heaped in front of them. The cafés give onto the open space where a small patch of earth has been leveled and planted with one or two mulberry trees, stunted before they could yield fruit. Urbanization creeps along the canal, parallel to it, separated from it by a dirt track three feet wide. Where the digging of the canal stops, construction stops too, and the halt may last for many years.

The water flows from the river into the canal in the morning when the gate of the canal lock is opened for a few hours, before it is closed again. Sometimes the water is low in the canal. The locals go down with their buckets and pots and trudge through the sludge to the meager water settled in the bottom. They look for Afifi to open the gate of the lock and wait for him on the wayside if he is on some errand. He usually tells them that he cannot open the gate, because the water is also low in the river, and he says that these are his orders and should anyone from the government pass by—and someone always does—and see the gate open in an off hour, "What do you think would happen then?"

As he sits astride his small she-donkey, his legs, uncovered by the drawn gallabiya, are folded to the sides so his feet do not touch the ground. They walk alongside him silently. When he reaches his home, he looks at them, clamping his toothless mouth and crinkling his face. "And even if I opened it all day long . . . "

Then staring angrily at the faces close to him, he says, "All right. I leave it to God." He turns his mount around in the midst of the crowd and heads back toward the lock to open it.

When the digging of the canal resumes, construction continues too. Finally, the waterway stops, having almost reached the lake. It ends with an elevated concrete dam.

The houses overlook the lake, separated from it by a wide stretch of arid land covered in a thin, brittle crust of salt, interspersed with reed shoots that quickly wither and brambles which the gusts of wind uproot and smash against the houses and the tracks.

The town is over there in the lap of the river, two miles away from the lake, shaded by willow and eucalyptus trees. On both sides of the river are spacious houses with columns, terraces, and façades painted in colored stucco, and beyond the houses are narrow, winding lanes and alley-ways.

For years, as the new settlement extended toward the lake the town continued to supply all its needs. After their canal was built, the big merchants switched from the cotton trade to trading in land—a trade which flourished after the canal was dug—as well as cement, timber, and steel construction bars. Through the generations they had acquired that keen, far-sighted outlook. Standing at the wide stretches of arid land, they saw in the area the natural extension of the town. They bought dirt cheap before anyone else took note, and left the area until they felt like undertaking new endeavors.

The people of the lake come to the canal for their water. Some of them who come from distant islands navigate for half a day in their sailing boats to reach it. They usually arrive in the mid-afternoon. They say that the canal in our town differs from the ones in other towns overlooking the lake, in that it has reached so close to the shore that they do not have to walk long on land carrying the water barrels.

They fold the sails and push the boats until their sterns sink into the mud of the shore. They roll the empty water barrels in front of them on the tracks their feet have made amid the arid land. The pieces of clothing that cover them are few and tattered. While some of them go to nearby shops to purchase their supply of sugar, tea, tobacco, and halvah, others proceed with the barrels to the canal.

After loading the boats, they sit on the lake shore

around a small fire, smoking water-pipes, wolfing down the halvah, and throwing the empty boxes into the boats. In an hour or two, they leave.

Seldom do we see them in the town streets, even on market days. Long months may elapse before we see three or four of them selling a calf in the market. We single them out from others who have come from nearby towns by their sun-burnt complexions, their steady, placid gazes and hesitant gait. They are not used to the long gallabiyas they wear when they come to town. The hems twist around their legs with every gust of breeze and hamper their movements. They always choose a spot remote from the throng of the market, usually somewhat elevated. Propped on their arms against the back of the calf, they pay no attention to the din around them, not even bothering to respond to provocations from the urchins who prowl the market looking for mischief. They name a price and stick to it. As the market grows more crowded, they do not budge from their spot. They half listen to buyers' attempts to bring down the price of the calf, then turn away. When the sun descends toward the other side of the sky and the crowds begin to disperse, they remain standing in their spot. The market is about to disband. The buyer who offered a slightly lower price merely out of a desire for bargaining lingers nearby, expecting them to call him. As they walk past him on their way back to the lake, he whispers his consent to their price, but for some reason they refuse to sell to him and continue on their way, drawing the calf behind them.

*

The islands are numerous in the lake: large, dark areas of little prominence that have not fully shaken off the moisture. The water rises with the flow of the tide at night and covers large parts of their shores. With the advent of day, the tide will have ebbed, leaving behind pools full of water and a few agitated fish. The sides of the islands slope gradually. They are covered with dark green weeds and small blooming reeds with sap that oozes in sticky drops on the slender stalks. Many cattle graze, sometimes straying along the sloping sides into trails of weeds, and when they find themselves unable to return, they start to low loudly. Slender boats come ashore amid the reeds in the shallow waters, bobbing with the rhythmic movement of the waves.

The lake waters deepen farther away from the islands, sometimes revealing a dim protrusion that extends underwater in a graded slope: dark weeds on its sides undulate with the currents, and wavelets collide above. It is just an island awaiting the waters to recede from it.

Before it arrives, they talk about the sea gale as something they always expect. Its omens loom on the horizon: the waves of the expectant sea and the languid waves of the lake, which, as if touched by a tremor, come and go, their even course disarrayed, before settling for an inward direction toward the shores and the islands. A stillness suddenly reigns over the lake's surface, as if it is holding its breath, and the sea's roar resounds from afar.

The gale comes sweeping, its echo resonating into the depth of the lake. The sea waves invade the channel—mountains of frothy water chasing each other—at which the banks of the channel crumble. The waves of the lake swell and rise, and their motion intensifies. They clash, send spray, acquire shadows and wispy foam. Turbid water rises from the lake's bursting depths, inundating the weeds and green reeds on the sides of the islands. The water keeps surging as if it will never stop. Small islands that had started to emerge from the depths now disappear. The few houses on the larger islands—huddled on small patches for which elevated areas were chosen—appear to be floating on the surface of the water. Their owners stand in front with their cattle watching the water flow relentlessly toward them.

The gale always comes on time—somewhat later or earlier perhaps, but it always comes. The winter gale frightens us. That sudden stillness as if everything has stopped expectantly. Dense, somber clouds gather. Cold winds about to break out. A muffled sound, like a tremor in the entrails of the earth. Every time we tell ourselves it is just an imminent storm that will take its time and recede. Yet it remains hovering on the horizon. We hear its rumble but it does not come. We have a sense of emptiness and an obscure sadness weighs on us. The dogs on the doorsteps snarl but do not bark.

A fleeting gust of wind lashes us and goes. Another comes, and then another. In a sudden recovery the sky glimmers. The dark clouds seem to be gathering to move away. At nighttime we see the streets enveloped in a silvery light, and we say that this is one of its ruses to lure us out of our hiding places. The soft light fascinates us. We drop our guard and go out, induced by the sense of security that the light has diffused around us. A warm, gentle breeze is in the air, and a stillness we dare not breach with our voices. The blast comes unexpectedly—the clattering of the sky, the profuse rain, the clamorous roar of the sea. Mighty waves that have long twisted soundlessly rush out with a muffled rumble, swallowing the fallow land and running in the alleys amid the houses of the settlement. It is water with a black spume that hurls at us flotsam it has trailed from afar with carcasses and dead fish.

9

They usually came in the last quarter of the night when the gale had reached its peak and the rain was still falling violently and sweepingly. We found out after they had been here a number of times that they came from the islands. How could they navigate through the gale? Their slender boats could not have withstood it. Some said it was the wooden boards which skid smoothly on the waves. They took the familiar route across the lake that they were used to taking when they came to the channel with their empty barrels to stock up on water from the canal. Some of them, giving full rein to their whim, made their way to the sea through another outlet said to be in the distant part of the lake. They mounted the clamorous sea waves and, following a circular course like a wide bow, landed in the channel. Then the two groups met.

For several trips no one saw them, and when later they did, they said the men were in the rags they wore while fishing: half a linen gallabiya, frayed and sleeveless, clinging to their bodies and dripping with water. They appeared naked in the fleeting lightning. Carrying cudgels and iron bars, they darted through the alleyways. They flattened against the walls, panting and brandishing the cudgels and bars as if someone was about to take them by surprise. They hid on the brick benches in the doorways of houses. At intersections they stole glances right and left before they crossed. When they heard a sound they spread out and encircled the alley, eyes focused like cats, and crept into it from both ends, meeting in the middle then spreading out again.

Drawn by the lights seeping from one of the houses, they would head for it and break in with a rough kick on the door, which opened wide. Screams would burst out within. Their faces haggard, they would stand there panting, dripping with water, and staring into the terror-stricken, speechless faces turned toward them. And, as if they had not found what they were looking for, they would take several steps backward and vanish.

The first few times they made do with the new settlement. They would head from the channel toward it, roam through it, then leave and stand in the open space, buffeted by the wind and rain, the sea water flowing between their feet. They would stare at the houses that stood tamely resigned to the lashing of the winds, the thunderous downpours and the successive lightning flashes. Once again, they would return to break in, then leave and stand in the open space, panting and gazing at the houses.

Their raid would continue until the somber light loomed on the horizon behind heavy clouds. Then they would hold onto their wooden boards and leave.

Afterwards they found their way to town. Having finished with the settlement, they would maraud through its alleyways once or twice. Then they would dash toward the town along the canal, crossing the two-mile stretch that separates it from the settlement in a run, pursued by thunder and lightning. In the fleeting light they looked scattered between the few wide-spaced trees, with mud splattering around them. They would stand panting at the outskirts of the town, which appeared as silent, darkened blocks, deep in sleep, with rain streaming down on them. Charging into the wide market street that stretched ahead of them, they would scatter the empty crates and boxes they came upon in front of the closed shops, then disperse in the nearby alleyways. Screams would suddenly break out amid the storm. The locals near the street would come out, hindered by the downpour and the mud, and when they reached the spot of the screams they would find the men from the lake gone. We would stand in the alleys, listening out for their swift movements after the screams that broke out from time to time in different spots. We sometimes saw them flit across the intersections and went panting after them, lost amid the stormy weather. Before seeing them dart between us we would sense a panting snarl that scorched us and was gone. Finally, we would lose patience and lie in wait for them by the side of the road that leads to the lake. Time would pass without a sign of them. The dark, dense clouds screened the sky so we could not make out dawn when it approached. We would return exhausted and stand in front of the houses, whipped by the wind and heavy downpour. We said we've lost nothing. No harm has befallen anyone. Just a few broken doors, chairs, and crates. So let it be. We were terrified and it wasn't worth it, and if they want to run around in the storm, let them run as much as they please. Had we turned off the lights in the houses, no one would have felt their presence.

So we turned off the lights with the advent of the gale and lay low in our houses. We heard them when they came: the stamping of their feet in the mud, their snarl as they wandered tirelessly through the streets, and their panting breaths when they flattened against the closed doors.

"Why our town?" we wondered.

"It's where they got used to coming for their supply of water," some said.

The darkness thinned somewhat over the arid land in the open space. The mud was thick and the puddles wide. Some of the people of the settlement who had peered out of the doorways of houses to watch the flow of water in the alleyways saw them on their way back when they went out into the open space, wading through the heavy downpour, heading for the channel. No one was keen to follow them, maybe because of the rain and mud, or maybe because of their exhausted gait. They leaned on their cudgels, using them to test the depth of the puddles they came across. One minute they formed a ragged line that zigzagged to avoid the deep puddles, another they huddled together, walking slowly then pausing for a short while before moving on. And when lightning glimmered the locals saw the men from the lake looking around then dispersing, as if frightened by the glare.

<h2 style="text-align:center">10</h2>

Gomaa's wife used to go to the shore on the days of the gale. In early youth she had found a silver bracelet among the debris spewed up by the sea. She wore it on her wrist and never took it off, and though more than twenty years had passed since that day, she would still go out to the shore, never missing a gale. Her small house near the lake was stacked with fantastic objects picked from the shore: shells, hollow and flat; hard, colorful stones; bottles of different shapes and hues; empty cans; spoons; plates; knives; broken bits of chairs; deflated dinghies.

She would leave her house in the midst of the gale, slipping out unnoticed, into the gloom of the somber dawn, with an empty sack slung over her shoulders. When the catch was abundant the sack was quickly filled. Paddling home, she towed the sack in the water. Her husband, sensing her return, would be standing on the threshold, wrapped in an old quilt. He would take hold of one end of the sack. Preceding him into the courtyard, she would stand by the fire, wringing her wet gallabiya while he emptied the sack. Then she would return to the shore. But when the gale was niggardly, she could remain on the shore until midday and return with a sack only a quarter full.

Women neighbors saw her days after the gale wearing

new things. Once she wore leather slippers adorned with roses. Although the leather was cracked and the petals were broken, the slippers looked dazzling on her feet, which she had rubbed with a pumice stone. Another time, they who had never seen anything but black veils saw her in a soft, colorful, transparent one. They touched it in amazement, with its delicate colorful prints—red, yellow, green. True, they spotted its frayed edges and the tiny holes mended with thread similar to the thread they used. But all these defects became invisible once it was on her head and began to wave in the light breeze above her hair, which she had washed, parted in the middle, and braided for the occasion. She smiled at their glances and pulled the veil, holding it with her lips. And on her chest they saw beads of all shapes and colors, and also hairpins the like of which they had never seen, sometimes in the shape of a leaf, or a boat and a fish.

One day she went out to the town market with her husband. She wore a yellow knee-length silk dress with brown diagonal stripes and a zipper in the back. She also wore black boots. Her husband, riding the donkey, was in front of her. The women accompanied her for a little while. Her bare knees were dark and her calves had green bulging veins. They told her that the boots looked like a soldier's, but she paid no attention.

They said they were far too big, but she had inserted some stuffing in the toes, and so it did not bother her.

They said that the dress was frayed around the zipper and torn under the arms, that her stitches were obvious for all eyes to see. She quickened her step and caught up with her husband.

She took them to her house one day when Gomaa was in town. They had shown admiration for a green and yellow woolen waistcoat that she wore over her gallabiya. It was too tight for her, but it was lovely. On the right side of the chest it had a tiny pocket with a bead. The women gathered in the room and she pushed the door shut.

A small window close to the ceiling gave off a little light. They saw an old sheet draped over one part of the wall, apparently covering hanging objects, their prominence visible from underneath. They lifted the corner of the sheet to take a look but she pushed them away, saying that these were Gomaa's things that he did not like anyone to see. They moved toward a heap of things piled in a corner of the room, rummaging through the empty bottles and the shells. One of the women picked a red shoe with a high heel. She was examining it when Gomaa's wife took it and tossed it on the pile, saying, "There's only one . . . until I find its twin."

Gazing at them and laughing, she hitched up the gallabiya to her waist. They saw her panties, as small as the palm of a hand, barely covering anything at all. They squealed in wonder. The panties were soft to the touch and had a bright print. Pulled taut above her thighs, they made her curves look beautiful. They had strings forming two bows at the sides. She said that as soon as she pulls the strings, the panties fall of their own accord, then she pulled the string on either side and they saw the panties loosen in front and in the back. She said she had found two pairs in the last gale. Then she spun around and let down the gallabiya. Leading the way to the door, she said that not once did she pass beside Gomaa without his stripping her, and then she laughed.

They saw Gomaa, too, come out in new things after the gale. Once he wore shoes, and because he had never before worn shoes he walked sluggishly, lifting his feet more than necessary. Another time he wore brown sunglasses, and went on about the scorching sun that harms one's eyesight. In his hand was a rosary, the roundness of its beads and their color unlike any they had seen, and a small pen-knife sheathed in ivory that he would open to scrape a reed stalk or a stick. One day he went out with his sleeves rolled up, with a watch on his wrist that was full of water that shook under the glass—but then that would only take a few days to evaporate. And they saw plates made of a metal that does not rust. There was also a small rocking chair fit for a boy, which Gomaa's wife placed on the threshold of the house, saying it was for decoration, and a year later they saw the small table beside it.

They also saw a lantern with a slightly rusty net of thin wire encircling its round glass. Gomaa's wife hung it on a nail above the entrance to the house. Gomaa took it along whenever he went out at night to buy tobacco or stay up in the café. It had a knob on the side to turn down its flame. He would sit relaxed, the lantern by his feet, all eyes on him. Gusts of wind blew and the flame did not flicker. Gomaa spoke of the dark night, of the ditches and the animal dung and human feces that fill the alleyways. You smell them but can't make out where they are in the dark. You sense them when your foot sinks into them and they stick to it and move with it, and the moon doesn't help, because the moon doesn't come out when you need it, and it doesn't come out in lands that have incurred God's wrath.

Gomaa stopped the she-donkey in front of the doorstep of the house and put the saddle and the saddlebag on it. His wife went into the house and came out carrying things she stuffed into the two openings of the saddlebag. Then she put two chairs, a table, and a rubber boat on the donkey's back. Gomaa tied them with a rope, then cast an old cloak over them to hide them from the onlookers.

The women in front of the houses watched the goings-on. Every market day two or three weeks after the gale Gomaa and his wife loaded the she-donkey and crossed the two miles to town. Throughout the two weeks they would leave the fragments of chairs and tables that Gomaa's wife had found on the shore in the sun to dry. With some additions of bits of discarded wood, the chair and the table would take shape. He would polish the vessels and metal utensils with ash from the oven mixed with powdered red brick and a dash of oil so they regained their sheen, and he would even rub them with sandpaper when needed. He would mend the holes in the boats and the dinghies with an adhesive material a truck driver had brought him from town. For an entire day and night, he would inflate the dinghies then line them up in the entrance of the house.

The boat, which accommodated two, was blue and red. The dinghies were yellow and green. The children gathered and sat on the ground in front of the house, and Gomaa watched them delightedly, but when he eventually wearied of them and their insistence on trying them out in the lake, he deflated the dinghies.

They would cross the two miles to town early in the morning—he leading the she-donkey by the head, controlling its pace, she following it, carrying a big, laden basket. Gomaa would spread out his wares at the end of the market, at a distance from the crowd. The bottles attracted attention with their unfamiliar colors and shapes. Some had two handles, others a single one, and yet others were shaped like a small barrel with a handle on the side. His customers were teachers and government employees. They used the shells for stubbing out cigarettes, the cans to buy paraffin and oil in from the shop, and the exotic bottles for decoration on window sills and tables in guest rooms, while ordinary bottles were for refills of liquid medicine in the government hospital. The lighters and pens that did not work had their customers too. Turning them over, a government functionary would say, "It doesn't matter. Their look is enough."

They returned with the shadows of sunset. No one could see what they carried. Gomaa's wife carried the laden basket on her head, and he carried the saddle-bag with the full pockets on his shoulder across the doorstep, bent with its weight. They closed the door early. Not a sound was heard from within.

Early in the morning the women saw watermelon peels, a

carved melon, and bones scattered in front of the house. Turning over the bones with her big toe, one of them said, "Lamb."

"Yes, lamb."

"A leg. And a shoulder joint. This is a shoulder bone."

"Anyone hearing you would think you have lamb meat every day."

"Yes. In my father's house, before I got married."

"There's just him and her, they have no children—and they eat all this."

On summer nights Gomaa and his wife sit on two chairs placed on the doorstep, drinking tea. The lantern hanging from the peep window of the door above their heads gives off a pale light, surrounded by a swarm of mosquitoes. The teakettle, painted yellow, has letters in a foreign language engraved on its side. One or two neighbors passing by greet them and Gomaa asks them in for tea. They sit on the reed mats spread on the doorstep while Gomaa swings in the little rocking chair, his body crammed into it. His wife pours out tea for the guests. Gomaa chatters about how tea retains its flavor when the kettle is well-made, and curses the times that have brought the manufacture of utensils within the reach of all.

A cool breeze blows in from the direction of the lake, causing the lantern to sway.

"The foreigners—such clever bastards."

He spits to the side and adds, "When they make something, they make it tip-top."

"Gomaa is no longer as he was."

They find him distant and introverted, listening to them absent-mindedly and mumbling a meaningless word or two. He has adopted the posture of the sage and always has a grain of opium under his tongue. The odor reeking from his mouth hits them in the face.

They have come to notice that he no longer goes to the café. He spends his evenings on the doorstep of his house. His wife prepares the water-pipe for him, refill after refill. They glimpse the glow of the coal in the dark as he drags on it. There is a tray of roasted peanuts beside him and from the thresholds of their houses, they hear the crackling of the peel amid the prevailing silence.

No one had paid much attention to him before. Like many others, he goes to town in the morning, returning with the evening prayers. He has no craft or regular job—a day here, a day there. The town, full of cement and iron shops and timber warehouses, is always crowded with numerous trucks on the bank of the river awaiting their turn.

All day long he loads the trucks with iron rods and sacks of cement and plaster. Sometimes he has to work late into the night, and then he spends the rest of the night in the shop. Trucks make way for other trucks, and there is so much work it is unending. Work in the cement shop with its heavy suffocating dust exhausts him. When he has enough money to last for a few days, he suddenly shakes himself free. This can happen at the beginning of the day or half-way through. He leaves the shop, followed by the curses of the owner, and spends a day or two loitering amid the ceaseless bustle before returning to the settlement. He lies on the doorstep fast asleep, a shawl on his face. His wife rubs his back and whisks the flies off him.

When no bread is left in the house, he drags himself to town.

His wife says that his health is too frail, but no one believes her. They weary of her when she keeps up this kind of talk, for they have never heard him complain of any illness. They wonder what it is that makes her borrow left and right, leaving him lying on the doorstep like a ewe.

After the gale he revives and no one sees him. He remains hidden inside the house, the door closed, poring with his wife over the objects she has brought. They sort them out, putting on one side what they will sell in the market and on another what they will keep for their own use. The things that interest him he picks and puts beside him. Having learned the kind of objects that appeal to him, she brings them whenever she finds them, without disdaining them as she does many other useless things.

He now has a collection he hangs on the wall. On those nights when the weather is fine, he goes into the room, followed by his wife carrying the lantern. He has prepared some bedding for himself inside—a pillow and a reed mat covered in a lamb's wool cloak. The room reeks of a moldy sea smell that emanates from the objects. Still damp in a far corner are dark green weeds that his wife has removed from the objects.

Gomaa sits cross-legged on the bedding, his wife seated beside him with her legs folded in. They usually wash before going into the special room, and each dresses in a clean gallabiya. The scent of perfumed soap wafts from her, and her short, frizzy hair glistens with moisture. They drink tea in silence.

Gomaa gently pulls the sheet off the wall. A sword hangs from its handle slightly tilted, its tip propped on a nail. The sheath is covered with many motifs, their color faded but for tiny yellow and red spots. The metal handle has lost its sheen. Gomaa draws it out slowly: half a sword with a blunt blade. He puts his hand through the handle and tightens his grip. With his fingers resting in the smooth groove, he brings the handle close to his wife's nose and says, "The smell of its owner's sweat—even though hundreds of years may have passed. Who do you think was the last to hold it?"

"Who?"

"I don't know. These decorations probably tell of him. He would have been a great warrior: only much fighting breaks a sword."

He passes his finger along the blunt blade. "And how many necks has it severed!"

He hands her the sword. She contemplates it for a moment then returns it. He puts it back in the sheath and rubs off with a rag the dust that has settled on it.

He picks up two pistols that are hung pointing in opposite directions.

"Decorations here too."

The handles of the pistols are of wood, their edges eroded. They carry decorations in relief. The barrel of one has a broken edge.

"All old things have many decorations," he says.

"And nice ones."

"They were carefree. Plenty of patience. They worked with gusto. These decorations are not bad at all. They tell of them and their times. At school they now teach how to decipher their secrets. These days all things look alike. Look," he shows her one of the handles, "a short line, a slanting line, a zigzagging line, and a circle. They must be signs that were known in their time. Its owner engraved them. And here too. They look like two letters. As I learned, some used to put the first letter of their names on their objects. The other," he shows her the handle of the other pistol, "has no letters on it. Its owner seems to have been like us."

"The best of people."

"Yes. When his pockets empty, he sells or pawns it. After a few days he retrieves it. Time and again, until someone kills him."

He draws a shield from the wall and places it on his arm.

"They used to fight face to face."

The shield has sustained a powerful blow that split its side. Rust has corroded its edges and reached to its middle, effacing some of the details of an engraving on the surface, of which only the outstretched wing of a bird has remained intact.

"Steel. Solid steel. How could it have rusted? Only an axe could gash it. And what a blow. It betrayed its owner. Was he on horseback? Or maybe on board a ship, or on foot."

"On horseback."

"Why the horse?"

"So he can escape."

"He'll never fight after his shield is broken. He throws it away. What use is it to him? He's lighter without it, holding the bridle with both hands. The other man won't catch up with him."

He returns the shield to its place on the wall and takes hold of a piece of chain mail, not unlike the net of a sieve. He turns it over in his hands, absorbed in silence. Leaning her arm on his thigh, she whispers, "If only it were intact."

"What use would it have been to us, if it were intact? Who fights with a sword these days? Scratches and gashes—what's wrong with them? Each scratch or gash has a story that distinguishes it. They give it a flavor."

He appears to her other than the Gomaa she knows. Where does he get all this talk? Her eyes are pinned on his pale face, which flushes when he gets excited. His eyes glow, and a bulging vein pulsates on his neck. She wishes she could touch it when it swells and its pulsing quickens, but she fears he would recoil at her touch. She does not like his objects. Things are beautiful when they are of some use, but everything he collects is of no use. Even if he were to display them in the market, no one would buy them. But these are the moments when he is good-humored. He sits her beside him, and they chat and laugh together. His hand pets her face and breasts. He sometimes pulls her toward him and caresses her body. She wards him off. Every time she yields to him in this room, she senses him distracted in her embrace. "They're watching us from the wall," he suddenly murmurs.

He picks up three pipes he has hung from their bowls and pushes their stems toward her.

"The teeth of their owners. They would grip them with their teeth while talking. And the saliva. Here's the mark of their saliva. See, the color is faded."

He has lined against the wall a porcelain vessel with broken handles and some earthenware pots with chipped edges.

"And here too. The mark of the scraping of the spoon, and maybe of their nails. And this black hue on the side. The food must have got burnt on the fire."

He puts out his hand and brings the talisman, as he calls it, from the wall where it is hung at some distance from the other things. There are four beads, two black ones on one side and two blue ones on the other, strung together on a cord of twined hair. His fingers feel it.

"Tail hair. It's the toughest. Its fiber is strong."

"A horse's tail?"

"Maybe of animals we don't even know."

In its center is the face of a beast with bared tusks, carved in wood tinted black. The two sharp, protruding tusks are a yellowish white.

"Made of bone?" she asks.

"Or maybe of the teeth of an animal. Big rats."

He puts it in his palm and brings it closer to the lantern.

"From what I've heard, they used to hang them around their necks to ward off harm," he says.

"A talisman?"

"They lived amid the trees. Atop them, beneath them.

What use would a talisman be? Swords. Pistols. Beasts."

"When I saw it I was afraid to touch it. I let it go, then went back to it saying, maybe Gomaa would want it."

He takes up the medal. Made of silver, it is large, the size of a twenty-piaster coin. It hangs from a piece of faded red cloth with frayed edges. Carved on it is the face of a man whose features are eroded.

"A medal. Victories. Swords glimmering, slicing off heads."

Finally he brings the stone from the small shelf. He always keeps it until last. It is the size of half a brick, the dull color of sandstone, rough with one even side. She recalls the day she brought it.

"I didn't see the writing on it. I thought I'd rub my feet with it."

The writing is etched on the even side, divided by a straight vertical line. That day Gomaa rubbed the even side with a tile so that it became smoother, and cleaned the grooves of the letters with the tip of a nail. When she suggested that he paint half the writing in red and the other half in blue, he would not listen. "We'll leave it the way it is," he said.

He brings the stone closer to the light of the lantern and runs his finger along the letters.

"Amazing letters," he says.

"Could it be true, Gomaa?"

He turns to her, and she asks, "Could it be true that these are words they write on tombs?"

"Who said so?"

"You did, two days ago. You said they wrote their names on tombs."

"I said so? Pass your finger over it."

She passes her finger over the letters.

"The first part has small letters," he says. "Their groove is narrow and deep."

"Yes."

"And the second . . . "

"Has big letters."

"And elongated."

"Yes, elongated. And the carving is on the surface."

"It's different from the first part. It must be that two people did the writing."

"The second was written by a woman. Yes, a woman. She bides her time lengthening the letters. And her hand isn't strong enough to carve deep."

"Fine. And the first?"

"The first was by a man. He carves as he will. And he has a lot to say."

"Perhaps they wrote at the same time."

"Yes. They were together. A man and his wife."

"And why would they write on a stone if they were married?"

"Ah."

"They entrust their secret to the stone, attach it to a rock, then go their separate ways."

"And never see each other again?"

"They wrote it when they knew they wouldn't be seeing each other again."

"A word here, a word there."

"Even the ends of the letters are incomplete. They didn't care to extend them a little."

"They resemble cracks in the wall."

The stone is in his palm. He puts it back on the shelf and the two of them gaze at it for a while in silence. He lets down the sheet and draws it over the other objects lined by the wall.

She asks him if he would like some tea. He says he does not want any.

They sit by the plate of hot coals.

With his eyes on the flames, he whispers, "When I look at them for a long time, it seems to me they're about to speak, to talk like we do. Yes, they look like they want to talk. Maybe if we give them some time."

They said that even after he had found his way to the market and had known what it was like to have money, he remained the same pleasant Gomaa they had always known—chatting with them in the evening about people who inhabited the past, while they listened attentively and in wonder.

But ever since his wife came across the chest his whole being changed. He was no longer the Gomaa they had known. His wife later said that had she known that all this was going to happen, she would have let the waves carry the chest back into the sea. Every time she recounted the story of finding it, she added details they had not heard before. She had seen it shining and at first thought it was a broken glass: she sees so many bits of glass and it had the same luster. As she came and went, she had caught sight of it, but kept her distance. She could have gone home without it. Something, though, made her look back. A wave was approaching, and the water undulated as it flooded the shore. She would noticed the chest turning with the motion of the water. Her heart sank, though she did not know why. She retraced her steps. First, she poked it with her stick, but with each poke the chest eluded her. It sank and disappeared, but she remained fixed until it floated back. Finally, she stretched out her hand and pulled it out of the water. Then she opened it. It was empty. She did not hear the voice—the voice she would hear later, after Gomaa had dried it by the fire. Had she known then it had a voice, she would have thrown it immediately back into the sea.

Those who actually saw the chest with Gomaa were very few. One day, when he was on his way to town, they met him and stopped to chat. They noticed the thing wrapped in rags under his arm and guessed it was the chest they had heard about. At the time, he was still friendly with people, so they asked to see it. He wavered for a moment, staring at them, before removing the rag and handing them the chest.

It was small and rectangular, and the sheen of its metal was tarnished. It was adorned with engraved and embossed motifs. The corners and the handle were made of ivory. They put it on their palms, turned it over, touched its slender legs, then gave it back to him.

When he pressed a button on its side to open the lid, soft music flowed. They listened. Just as they were about to say something, he hushed them. The music stopped, and a mellow voice said something, then was silent. The voice hovered over them, its melancholy cadence like the dark, dense sea fog. They asked if it was the voice of a woman.

Gomaa said it was a man.

"What does it say?"

"Who knows."

He wrapped it again in the rag and said he was on his way to town to look for the English teacher to ask him about the meaning of the words. He looked distracted and haunted, so they said they would go with him as they had nothing else to do.

One of them thrust his she-donkey toward Gomaa. For an instant he eyed them hesitantly then rode it. The four of them put on their gallabiyas, which were folded on their shoulders, and walked beside him.

All the way he remained deep in silence, and they felt sorry for him when they noticed his pallor. They stood with him in front of the closed school door. The porter came out to them. When they asked him whether there was an English teacher in the school, he looked at them in astonishment.

"What do you want him for?"

"We just want him."

After scrutinizing them for a moment, he went back in and, before closing the gate, told them to ask at the secondary school.

They walked to the secondary school on the bank of the

river, and found the porter seated on a small chair in the entrance next to the half-open door. He told them that the teacher was in class, so they squatted beside him and waited.

When the teacher came out, he listened to the voice then closed the lid.

It wasn't English. "It may be French," he said, gazing at the chest.

He asked Gomaa if he would sell it, but Gomaa answered that he was not interested.

"What would you do with it?"

Gomaa, clutching the chest with both hands, asked if there was anyone at the school who knew French.

The teacher disappeared for a while then returned with three people.

They listened to the voice over and over, then one of them said it wasn't French.

"Not German, either," another said.

"Do you know German?" someone asked.

"A little. The pronunciation is different."

They passed the chest between them, whispering among themselves as they fingered the engravings. Gomaa gazed at their faces silently.

One of them commented that there were many tongues in the world.

Another said that women abroad keep their jewelry in such chests, and when they open them, music flows out. But he had never heard of chests that spoke.

They asked Gomaa once again if he would sell it, but he repeated that he would not.

On their way back from town, he said that this was what he had expected.

When they asked him what he meant by this, he said, "No one will be able to tell what the chest is saying."

He looked grim and said it was no coincidence.

"What coincidence do you mean, Gomaa?" they asked.

That the chest should fall into his hands, he said.

When they asked him what he was talking about, he looked at them angrily though they had said nothing that could have angered him. He glared at each one of them, as if about to swear, and said, "You will see. The time will come."

He walked away, widening his steps. They were taken aback by his anger, but caught up with him and walked beside him in silence. As they approached the settlement, he said, "Let's listen to the voice once more."

They stood in the shade of a tree by the wayside, and he opened the chest. In spite of the melancholy tone, the voice overflowed with vitality, reminding them of the rush of water in canals when the dams are opened. The same sheen, the rippling sound their ears picked out while standing in the midst of irrigation basins, a sound distinct from all others. The voice soared, and clung like a smell.

They said that every time they listened to it they imagined something different.

They also said that it drew them like a siren. Whenever they sensed they were about to grasp it, it suddenly eluded them, leaving them no peace.

They were approaching his house when he stopped abruptly and looked at them with that distracted gaze that was to become part of him. "If only we could understand the words," one of them said.

"It isn't important that we understand the words," Gomaa answered sharply. "No one will ever understand them. Only listen to them. Only listen."

He unwrapped the chest from the rags. As he gazed over their heads toward the sea his fingers sought the button. It seemed to them that the tone of the voice had changed, and only later did they notice they were close to the sea. The voice flowed, deep and tremulous, shadowed by a low murmur like sea waves undulating in the distance. And before the voice fell silent, Gomaa suddenly left them and went home.

"Him and his chest."

Standing there, they appeared as if they were waking from a heavy sleep. They followed him with their eyes until he disappeared into his house.

Days later the English teacher arrived in a horse-drawn carriage. He was accompanied by the French teacher and another, older man with a gray, pointed beard and a sagging jacket. It was afternoon when the carriage, trailing behind it many of the inhabitants of the area, stopped in front of Gomaa's house.

Gomaa's wife went out to meet them. She glanced at them and disappeared into the house. Then Gomaa stepped out, and she stood behind him in the doorway. Gomaa appeared at a loss as he gazed at them. It seemed that his wife had woken him from his afternoon nap.

The English language teacher said that the guest had heard of the chest and had come to see it. In a proud tone, he added that the guest was the district inspector of English, that he knew many languages and had traveled abroad.

There was something unfamiliar about the guest, possibly the great pleasure he appeared to be taking in being with them, and the glances he kept casting here and there, as if he had come upon something rare. He stroked the faces of the children standing around him and touched their hair, looked in astonishment at the lake, the sea, the stretch of arid land, and the façades of the houses.

"An amazing spot," he whispered to the English language teacher.

"What spot?" the English teacher asked.

"The confluence of the sea with the lake. And when will one get the chance to visit these places?"

They looked at Gomaa. Fragile and pale, he stood on the doorstep, leaning against the wall. The English teacher told him to fetch the chest. Gomaa looked at the guest's pipe, which gave out delicate smoke.

Two of the neighbors who had quietly slipped out from the crowd returned with three chairs and a table. The guest and the two teachers sat down, and the neighbors asked them what they would like to drink. The two teachers said they did not want anything, but the guest said, "What do you have?"

"Anything you may want."

He laughed merrily and said, "Tea."

The English teacher turned and, seeing Gomaa still standing in his place, told him to bring the chest. Gomaa asked the guest if he could look at his pipe.

The English teacher looked embarrassed, but the guest handed the pipe to Gomaa. It was burnished and shiny, with a gilded cover to its bowl, and its smooth, polished stem was slightly curved. Gomaa turned the pipe over in his hand, gave it back to the guest, looked at the English teacher and said that he had no chest to show anyone.

Stunned by what Gomaa had said, the English teacher suddenly leapt to the doorstep, glowering, and wanting to strike him, but the French teacher grabbed his arm.

Gomaa turned, went back into the house, and closed the door.

"He and his chest are in the house."

The voice resonates into the wide space, its tones tremulous, rising and falling, soaring far off with the wind. In the still night they hear it on the doorsteps. They say he is there by his darkened window with his arm resting on the sill, as they usually see him whenever they pass that way.

They see the window empty and linger a while. They hear the chest's voice within and see the black posters of the bed, rusty, their paint cracked. The shreds of a mosquito net hanging from the tips of the posters are encrusted with sticky dirt, fly droppings, and chicken feathers. If they stand on tiptoe to peer into the room, they can see a big black box along the wall, with loaves of bread visible through its open lid and a heap of clothes piled on it, among which they make out one of Gomaa's gallabiyas and a black veil that belongs to his wife. They also glimpse by the door the earthenware plate full of ash. Gomaa is in the corner of the bed close to the window. He shuts the chest when he sees them. They turn to him, exchange glances among themselves, then move away.

His wife sits on the doorstep, looking through the half-open door into the empty space. The voice of the chest reaches her. He opens it and closes it, day after day.

"Damn the chest and the day it came," she grumbles in a low voice.

He is sitting in bed, gazing absently through the open window at the wide space, with the chest beside him. He is immersed in the voice, as if seeking out what its tone conceals. He says it approaches then recedes, almost lights up then dims.

His wife, sitting on the doorstep watching a rolling ball of dry weeds, mutters, "Oh Gomaa, what has happened to you? Where was it lying in wait for you?"

She pushes the door against a chilly gust of wind, then pulls it open again. Gomaa's voice reaches her from the room, "Cover me, woman."

She sees him huddled in a corner, shivering. She closes the window, wraps him up in the quilt and cloak, lights a fire in the earthenware plate, then returns to the doorstep.

Later, he recovers his strength somewhat and goes out. He has learned by heart what the chest says, murmuring it as he walks. Their curiosity kindled by his long disappearance inside his house, they ask him when he passes by them, "Hello,

Gomaa. It's been so long. What does your chest say, then?"

He gives them a fleeting glance and smiles to them a little, or sometimes does not smile. Then he widens his perturbed steps, as if escaping the inquisitive eyes pinned on his face. Wrapped in his shawl, his shoulders are stooped. His arrogance and sense that he can do what he pleases are diminished. Quieter and more tolerant now, he contemplates serenely the wide leaves in the palm of his hand, tracing with gentle fingers their delicate veins. He sits square-legged on the banks of canals, watching the short leaps of frogs and schools of small fish darting between the weeds in the water.

For days he keeps away from the chest then returns to it. He has now taken to sitting in the front room instead of the bedroom, by his things hanging on the wall. He places the chest amid the pots under the sword hanging aslant. Lying relaxed, he gazes at the chest and his hand feels the engravings.

He spends the greater part of the day at home, replaying the voice time and again, exhaling silently, his feet folded, his toenail scratching the floor. His wife stands at the closed door, listening for a little while.

"Oh Gomaa, where is all this going to end?" she says.

The gale approaches. Its omens loom on the horizon. He paces up and down inside the house, as if feverish. He stands on the doorstep, gazing to the somber horizon, and whispers in a voice his wife overhears in the courtyard, "All the time it lay on the bottom, and when it came out, it came to no one but me."

His wife mends the tears in the sack she will take to the shore during the gale. She draws in her legs out of his way. She senses in the tone of his voice that he wants her to talk with him. But his angry outbursts in the middle of a conversation and his insults make her keep her mouth shut, though his state does not please her, nor would it please anyone, and how many times does she find herself on the point of saying it but holds her tongue.

"Years and years. People come and people go. It roves the world's seas—once here, once there. Its story is unending. Did you think its story had ended! You'll see."

He returns to the room and closes the door. Shortly afterwards the voice of the chest reaches her.

Gomaa's wife is woken by his voice. Something about it is unfamiliar. Lying there, she waits for the voice to recur. During the last few days, he often talked, alone in the front room, night after night. She would listen for a while, then doze off.

The fire by the door of the room is dying, and the shadowy rays of dawn are seeping in through the chinks in the window. From the room at the front she hears the voice of the chest with a ring she has never heard before and a stern, threatening tone. She says it is that voice that woke her up. The voice of her husband follows, low and husky.

"And who would I be?"

She listens attentively. Then comes the voice of the chest. A ringing overshadows the piercing tone of the voice, before it falls silent. Then comes the sound of light wind outside, a rat scratching under the closed door of the front room, from where a glimmer of light can be seen. Then the voice of her husband, murmuring, as when he is asleep beside her, dreaming.

"Yes. I like what you are saying."

He falls silent for a short while then whispers, "The sword. The talisman. The medal. All of them. I look and my mind wanders. People are the same everywhere, and what could change them? Countries disappear, others emerge. People go, others come. The sword. The medal. Has anything really changed?"

She can almost see him lying on his side, leaning on his arms, his knees drawn to his belly.

"When I heard your voice, it was as if someone were calling me. Alas, the teachers said they could not understand your speech. When they took you from me to listen, I could feel you not wanting to leave my hand, but I said to myself: Gomaa, wait, wait."

Silence again. Then the voice of the chest whispering, with no ringing this time, though its tone remains stern. Her husband is agitated; she can hear his sigh and angry murmur. He must have sat up suddenly, looking around him.

"Who do you think I am?" he says.

She can almost hear his heavy breathing. She knows he will calm down soon, grope the things around him and then lie down. The sound of a light cough reaches her.

"Why should you bother about people? Whether they become corrupt or not? And suppose they do? Will anyone have pity on them? On the lake, on the shore, in town, wherever. And what would they do? It's easy to talk. Oh how much you talk!"

His voice rises and falls, as if he is turning in his prone position. He cannot bear to lie on one side for long. Soon, he lies on his back with his hands under his head, his feet crossed. When sleep does not come he swings his foot.

"And how could you possibly know? For hundreds, perhaps thousands of years you've been lying on the bottom. How could you possibly know? How many times did you emerge? How many heads have you seen rolling under the sword? How many have you seen spitting blood? It was after he had carried sacks of cement. Gobs of blood coming out of his mouth in a dark corner of the shop. I carried him on my shoulders to the cart. He hadn't seen the blood until we were in the light.

"'It's blood, Gomaa.'

"Yes. It was blood. And the horse would not move.

"'My gallabiya is inside, in the shop, Gomaa.'

"'I'll fetch it.'

"Try and find a gallabiya in the dark. And the horse, hearing the barking of the dog, would not move. Who gives a damn about what you are saying. People have already had enough. Do you think they care for what you are saying?"

The ringing of the chest becomes very loud, overshadowing its voice. She can hear Gomaa groaning, "Why are you getting angry? Why? No sooner do I say something not to your liking than you get angry. The least thing angers you. You're unbearable."

Their two voices mingle until one cannot be distinguished from the other. Then Gomaa's voice is heard above the chest's. He is almost shouting. The veins of his neck bulge when he shouts. He must be standing up now, stretching his long neck, staring at the objects hanging on the wall, avoiding looking at the chest.

"Yes, I heard you," he says. "I already know by heart what you are saying. I repeat it to myself dozens of times every day, while walking in the streets, while at home, while eating, while drinking, even before sleeping. And now, you test me? What is it that you are saying? What is it, really? Fine, I'll never pay attention to what you say again."

Then she hears movements in the other room, as if he is walking to and fro, shoving the fallen bottles with his foot. She gets up, feeds the fire with bits of corn cobs and fans it until the flame flickers. She knows that he will eventually come to lie down beside her, cold and trembling, seeking her warmth. Every time he comes out of the room, she is alerted by his cough. She sees him shriveled in the light of the lamp he carries in his hand. He walks slowly to the courtyard, pauses in front of the wall, and feels with his hand for the nail on which he hangs the lamp. Then he returns, casting a glance inside the room he has just left. On his way to bed, he feels the warmth of the fire. He turns back, placing his hands above the flames. He stands erect, as if he has recovered his body. Is it the little warmth, or his regained awareness of things around him?

She holds him tight to her, tucks the cover around him, and rubs his back, until his shivering ceases. For some time, he will keep away from the front room, leaving it locked. In the morning he will go to town to look for work. It will seem then as if he has deserted the chest forever. He will spend the evenings sitting with her on the doorstep. Two or three days will pass, and then he will go back to the front room. He will ignore her when she calls. Then she will see his fury mount, and watch him come out of the room staggering. She will be sitting on the doorstep of the house, looking through the half open door into the empty space, where the wind has just calmed.

"This chest will not let go until it finishes him."

A not too distant day will come when he leaves for a place where none can find him. His wife will give him two loaves of bread, a chunk of cheese and two onions, thinking—now that he no longer tells her where he goes—that he will be late coming home. She stretches out her hand with the food and remains at the doorstep, waiting for him to receive it, and when he is through with saddling the donkey he takes it from her and puts it in the saddle-bag. It surprises her somewhat to see him take the chest, in the same rag he has wrapped it in since she found it. He draws the donkey, enveloped in silence, a strange serenity in his movements. He pays no attention to his surroundings while getting on his donkey, and when he reaches the top of the alley, he disappears. His wife tightens the veil around her head and closes her door.

And it will be seven years before she sees him again, emaciated and ragged, the skin of his face wilted and shriveled, the bones jutting out. He will be accompanied by a man with a long stick. The settlement will have changed, with many tall buildings covering the arid land and screening off the shore. His eyes search in vain for the landmarks he is accustomed to seeing. The ends of tall steel bars loom from beyond the houses. His house has receded and its brick bench is partly in ruins. There are sinuous cracks in the walls, some restored with cement, others still gaping. The façade is stained with dust and dirt the rain has carried down from the roof. He looks at his wife, who has aged in his absence, but does not utter a word.

They arrive in the late afternoon, when the sun is about to set and a chilly breeze is in the air. His wife stands on the side of the brick bench that is still intact, leaning with her shoulder against the wall.

"You're back, Gomaa," she says quietly, taking him under the armpit to help him up the brick bench he cannot climb by himself, and laying him down in bed. His breathing is deep, as if he were relieved, and maybe seeking out the smell of familiar things. She covers him, as she always did, with the quilt and cloak, and lights a fire in the plate. His feverish eyes gaze at her in silence.

She sits with the stranger in the courtyard. He tells her that Gomaa wanted to die in his home, that they had walked across so many lands.

"Your house is far."

The stranger sits on the reed mat, with his legs stretched out. His face is the hue of rust, his feet flat and caked in tar and dry mud from the roads. She asks him about the she-donkey and the chest.

The stranger takes a sip, and then another, from the glass

of tea in his hands and rubs his feet so the mud crumbles off. He says he had heard about the chest before he met Gomaa, and when he met him he had neither donkey nor chest. Since then they have been together.

She asks him what Gomaa did, for she has no explanation for his departure.

When the stranger says that Gomaa had his own reasons which no one knows, she asks if he has not recounted anything.

He says that there was much he recounted, for there was much that he had seen, and he was unstinting in his telling. And he was loved by all who knew him.

"I never heard him say he regretted his departure."

He falls silent for a moment then says that Gomaa always spoke well of her.

She asks him what is keeping Gomaa from talking.

The stranger says that he had been talking but fell silent when they approached the town.

He asks her if he can see Gomaa's things that are in the room.

She says they have been in their place since he left.

Carrying the lantern, she leads the way to the room. He pulls the sheet aside and murmurs, "Ah. The sword. The pistol. And where's the medal? Ah, and the talisman."

He gazes at them for a while without touching them, then lets the sheet down.

He asks her where Gomaa sat listening to his chest.

She points to the spot where he is standing. He takes two steps back and looks around, then goes back to the courtyard. The evening prayer has passed, the night growing darker, and the voices outside receding as they sit silently in the courtyard. He rests his head against the wall and closes his eyes from time to time. A low murmur comes from the room, followed by a faint moan. She makes to get up.

"Let him die in peace," he says.

"Maybe he wants something."

"He doesn't."

She sits back. And it will seem to her that all this is unreal, even Gomaa himself. It is as if she has never known him.

The voice in the room finally falls silent. The stranger awakens from his slumber. He feels around him for his stick and gets up. She tells him to wait until daybreak, but he leaves.

11

The gale comes as clamorous as usual. Gomaa's wife goes out in the dim light of dawn with the sack slung over her shoulder. The weather is overcast. The stormy torrents which lasted for two days have abated, but the peels of thunder continue. The lake, its own sound muffled by the clatter of these other sounds, has yielded to the flow of the tumultuous waves. The sea water rushes past the shore into the stretch of arid land.

Women lurking in the doorways of neighboring houses see her skinny figure wading through the water and mud with her gallabiya rolled up above her knees. They charge after her. She senses their presence when she gets to the shore and the water reaches her thighs. She waits until they draw closer before going on her way. Their bodies sway in the water, which deepens as they advance until it reaches their bellies, and they feel the bottom move under their feet. They bend and spread out their arms. Startled by the ditches, they fall over and suppress their shrieks, as their hair and faces are drenched and they shudder. The warmth of the water in the bottom flows through their legs, and they shiver whenever they become aware of it, and their teeth chatter. Every now and then they pause, the water buckling around them, the waves rising and falling, spray glistening endlessly. The expanse of deep darkness beyond is suddenly dispersed by lightning. In the fleeting light, they see the huge waves that loom in the distance, gathering force. They look at the houses they have left behind and see them dim and unrecognizable. They progress. Scattered by the sudden lashes of water, they stumble but soon draw together, holding each others' hands, the black veils on their heads wet and sticking to their faces.

Ahead of them, Gomaa's wife moves effortlessly, as if the water parts for her. The veil on her head is light, untouched by a single drop of water. Her body sways only slightly to avoid a breaking wave she barely takes notice of. She slows down until they catch up, then signals to them to disperse. They gaze at her silently and huddle closer together.

It was their first time. That day, Gomaa's wife found the wallet floating in the shallow water, almost concealed by the weeds and murky foam. She let out a cry in spite of herself, and the women rushed toward her. They could tell from her movements that she wanted to escape with it, so they abandoned their caution, stumbling, turning over in the water, and getting up again. Farther away from the shore the water was less deep. They spread out and waylaid her. They were drenched through, weeds and shells sticking to their veils. Gomaa's wife paused, looked around, then headed in the opposite direction, but they dashed behind her and caught up with her.

They said they had spotted it before her.

She answered that they had been far away.

"We went out together and together we'll return," they said.

"We didn't go out together," she said.

They were surrounding her. The one closest to her stretched out her hand to the wallet, but Gomaa's wife stepped back, and clutched it desperately. Then blows rained down on her. She received them bent forward, with her face hidden.

"Twenty years—you've had your fill of the sea."

They twisted her hair and hurled her away. She fell into the water together with the wallet, and they plunged her head until she let go of it.

As she wiped the mud off her face, she saw them move away. The wallet, made of leather, was about half a meter long. Two metallic letters were affixed in one corner, and it was secured with a silvery clasp in a loop. Inside it were a pen, a pair of spectacles, a bronze key-ring with many keys, and papers that turned to paste the minute they touched them. In a small pocket they found an identity card with a man's picture stuck on it. They looked at it, giggled, splashed each other with water and ran along the shore.

That day they agreed to divide anything they found equally amongst themselves. They did not object when Gomaa's wife demanded a bigger share, since it was she who had led them to the shore and since she would find things they could not spot.

She told them that there were things that surfaced in the first days of the gale and returned to the sea if they delayed.

She also said that there were things found immediately after the gale, when the water receded, that were swept along with the sand back into the sea if they delayed. They were tiny things that were usually wedged in the sand with only an end glistening, she explained, pointing to the earrings she wore. They were of pure 24-carat gold, she explained. She had found one and kept it. Two years later she found its twin. They felt the earrings in her ears and found them heavy. The motif was the same in the two earrings.

"Its twin," they said.

"Yes, its twin. Nothing is lost in the sea," she said.

They go out on the second day of the gale as the wan light of dawn appears beyond the dense, laden clouds. They gather in front of Gomaa's house, each holding a stick. When the gale is violent, the sea water rushes amid the houses.

Each woman tucks the hem of her gallabiya in her drawers and wades into the water. With their sticks they test the depth of the invisible ditches. They leave behind the muddy lake shore, which, inundated as it is with water, they make out only by the tips of green reeds swaying in the wind. They spread out all along the sea shore. In the distance, massive rocks intersect the sea forming a jetty, enveloped in a dense fog and lashed by huge waves that explode in spray. They thrust the sticks under the murky surface of the water, where they turn and search. When the ends of the sticks collide with something, the women pull it out and throw it in a sack which one of them drags. Shells, bottles, garments. Gomaa's wife turns at their shrieks when they find something. She says they are as indiscriminating as cows, and that what they have collected is the very same stuff she left last gale: no one buys bottles with broken mouths, and these shells are flat and small.

Sudden waves throw them, but they hastily gather themselves up, wring the water from their hair and veils, and go on wading. They stop at the rocks. Their movements slow down before they reach the rocks, and they fall silent. Successive turbid waves rush and gather in one huge swell bound for the rocks, the sound of its collision and its splinter-like spray surging high.

One of them, taken by a shiver, says that the place is very cold.

"Yes. And scary," another answers.

They return.

Gomaa's wife was the first to see the corpses. Her practiced eyes do not pause at objects that have no use. She always leads the others. Only occasionally does she stretch out the stick under her arm to poke some object with its end. As for them, they turn over with their sticks anything they see, even the garbage bags they tear up searchingly.

The corpses were lying face down, their heads close together and their limbs spread out. Only one, which had drifted far, lay on its back, swaying more than the rest with the motion of the water. Weeds and shells had settled afloat in the hollows between the legs of the four corpses. The rags they wore were drawn back to the shoulders. The water flowed and ebbed, leaving foam and fine sand on the naked bodies. The full muscles of their broad shoulders were relaxed, as if they were in a slumber.

Standing by the stray corpse, Gomaa's wife whispered, "He's uncircumcised!"

They turned the other corpses onto their backs, then hastened home. They told the men that, from afar, they had glimpsed on the sea shore what looked like corpses. The men went out to the shore, then returned. They said that apparently this was the group that came by the sea route. Some swore to their wives that if they ever went out to the shore again they would divorce them. Amongst each other they whispered, "The sons of bitches—not even a pair of pants to cover their private parts."

"And uncircumcised."

"Yes."

"Who'd have believed it?"

The women stood in the doorways of houses while the men gathered in the courtyard of the café overlooking the open space, which was deluged with water. The weather was bleak. Morning and noon were indistinguishable. In the daytime the gale appeared less clamorous, and even the huge breakers sounded less tumultuous.

"If they haven't come before sunset to take the corpses, we'll hurl them back where they came from," they said.

"And if they drift back to the shore?"

"We'll see."

After every gale, they said they were not going to keep quiet about it, then the days passed and they forgot. This time, they seemed determined. They stood with their backs to the wall of the café, away from the rain water which dripped through the fissures in the palm-slab roofing of the courtyard. Their eyes were on the lake. The water covered everything, overtaking all the shores and small, scattered islands they were accustomed to seeing. The sea overflowed into the lake unhindered.

"For years we've been putting up with them."

"Yes. There's a limit to everything."

"And where do they hail from? You don't know. Here and there. Neither an origin nor a land, nor a family—nothing at all."

"And they've survived a long time—a whole generation, now hatching the second."

"Our grandfathers used to count them on the fingers of two hands, saying, 'They won't bear up.' Let them come now and see."

They surmised it was afternoon when they saw a big boat without a sail emerge from the darkness of the lake, pushed with poles by some men. The men seemed to know the boundaries of the channel, which had become invisible. They stopped the boat away from the sea and stepped down. Two of them stood holding onto the sides of the boat. The four others advanced a little with the water reaching up to their bellies, then stopped and looked around them. From the café, a man shouted out, with his hands placed trumpet-like in front of his mouth. When they looked toward him, he gestured to where the corpses were. One after the other they turned and disappeared at the sandy bend in the shore. A while later they reappeared, each carrying a corpse on his shoulder. They put the corpses in the boat then turned once again, though they did not go far. They plucked out reed stalks from the depths of the water, brought their loads back to the boat, and scattered them inside.

The boat skimmed toward the distance and was swallowed by the dense fog that crouched on the lake.

The gale finally receded, leaving behind deep puddles, narrow rivulets, tree branches, bloated carcasses, and fish that were leaping when the ducks and geese rushed to snap them up. The clouds crept into the distance and a pale sun shone.

It was a warm day. The men in the café glimpsed the sail while it was still far in the middle of the lake. They set aside whatever they were doing and turned in their seats. Inflated with air, the sail approached slowly. It was on a small boat. The men on board pulled down the sail, folded it, and headed for the channel.

Our men got up and rushed to the shore. The women

came out of the houses and stood on street corners, while some men who had been lying on thresholds got up and widened their steps to catch up with the others.

The boat came ashore in the channel. Men with empty barrels stepped down from it. They rolled the barrels in front of them across the strip of arid land along the winding track, which was damp and hardly visible in the wake of the gale.

There were five of them, walking side by side, wrapped in their gallabiyas. Our men walked for a short while, then stopped and waited for them. "Take them back," they called out when they saw that the others were within earshot.

They went on shoving the barrels with their feet. Again, our men shouted out, "Take them back."

They halted the barrels with their feet, exchanged glances, then looked at our men. Leaving the barrels, they advanced.

"What's up?"

"Go find yourselves another canal."

"What happened?"

"Whatever happened."

Their elder, old and gaunt, said laughingly, "Someone must have angered you."

Some of our men snarled, and no one answered. Our men were grim, but did not wish to appear to be complaining. They stood blocking the way. The old man said that for years they had been taking water from our canal, and no one had opposed them.

"And now you come and say . . . "

"Yes, we say."

The old man took the gallabiya off his shoulders and shook it out. He seemed about to put it on, then put it back on his shoulders.

"For years we've been coming . . . "

They stood silently for a long while, and it seemed to be the end. The men from the lake turned and looked at the boat. Some of our men squatted. Neither group wanted to move. There was a chill in the air as they stood around quietly and thoughtfully. Suddenly the old man muttered, as if talking to himself, "Yes. Years."

"Yes. Years. And so what!"

"Nothing."

One of our men leapt forward grumbling. He said we had put up with them long enough, for they had no regard for any sanctity. They come naked. He agitatedly told of their running through the alleyways and the corpses we found.

The old man listened calmly. He said that there are many islands in the lake. Pointing to the long pants they wore, he said, "Did we ever come without these?"

Looking at our men one by one, he said, "How many times have we come here. You see us every time. We buy things from the shop. Did you once see us without them?"

"And uncircumcised," one of our men muttered, waving his arms.

The men from the lake exchanged glances. "Choose whoever you like," the old man said.

There was a heavy silence.

It was a fleeting instant, almost hallucinatory. The faces were awe-struck, as if they had suddenly stopped on the edge of a precipice. Later they recalled what happened wonderingly. A word from the old man would have put an end to it, they said. But as they had all guessed that the situation would not develop into a fight, they let the words carry them away. They only came to when the old man said, "Choose one."

He and his men stood upright, as if ready to comply with whatever our men saw fit, but their faces spelled defiance. And until this moment it was possible for one of our men to put an end to the situation with a word—but for Abdel Samie, that insolent one always squabbling with the women, who hurl mud at him whenever he passes them on the canal. He went berserk when he heard what the old man said and growled furiously, "What! What!"

He pushed aside the two men standing in front of him and, his arm shooting out violently, pointed to a youth standing behind the elder. He was the youngest, and his face showed signs of anger.

Abdel Samie, followed by one of our men, advanced to escort the young man, who remained standing, looking at them, motionless. "Go with them," the old man said.

The young man made no move and his eyes were pinned on Abdel Samie's face. Again, the old man said, "Go with them."

The young man suddenly turned and moved away. Abdel Samie and his companion followed him. They walked almost all the way to the shore. There, the young man pulled down his long pants. Abdel Samie and his companion returned, leaving him to make his way back to the boat.

On their way back, Abdel Samie suddenly turned, followed by his companion. They waded through the thick mud in the stretch of arid land. The men watched the two of them as they pulled up their gallabiyas. They walked on, with the mud reaching halfway up their legs, heading for the houses.

Our men turned back. The men from the lake followed, rolling their barrels and saying, "There are so many islands. They must be from farther up the lake."

"Yes. There they directly face the sea. And the currents surrounding them are violent."

"No one suffers from them like we do."

"They leave no one in peace and do not settle down themselves."

"You in your homes here know nothing of what is happening on the lake."

Our men reached the café and stepped up to it while the men from the lake went on rolling their barrels to the canal.

The gale comes and goes. It leaves behind whatever it leaves. The turbid water that covers the vast expanses of arid land along the shore soon dries up. The garbage is scattered by the wind. There are fewer and fewer corpses from one gale to the other.

"The sea will rid us of them," our men say.

The weather clears and the lake calms after the sea waves

recede. The waves of the lake chase each other languorously. The shores and small, verdant islands, which have reemerged, shake off the moisture. A new fragile crust of salt covers the arid land. It appears virginal, as if no foot has trodden it.

Wilderness

12

They talk about the sea gale for days after it has passed, then forget about it. When mention is made of the losses that have befallen the inhabitants of the settlement, they say Karawia the café proprietor and Afifi the grocer are the hardest hit. They see the two of them wading through the water and mud, then stopping not far in the midst of the open space with their gallabiyas rolled up. Karawia and Afifi stand still, looking out to sea, where the waves have calmed, bewildered by what has happened.

The café and the shop occupy the two corners of a narrow street that gives onto the open space. The café, with its wide courtyard, juts out slightly from the row of houses. Karawia and Afifi come together in the early morning and exchange talk across the narrow street while they open the café and the shop. Karawia brings out the chairs and tables, and lines them in the courtyard. Afifi pushes aside the barrels of oil and paraffin, and sweeps the brick bench of the shop.

They have their morning tea together, then neither sees the other until the end of the evening. At night, Afifi makes do with the light from the café, which extends into the shop. The hour being late, he sits on a chair struggling with sleep, wrapped in his cloak, waiting for Karawia so they can return together.

When the omens of the gale loom, Karawia shuts the café, since its customers are dispersed by the signs of the impending storm. With the weather overcast and the sea's roar resounding, he forgets in his haste to put out the lantern hanging behind the counter. After bringing the chairs in from the courtyard, and sprinkling water on the glowing cobs, he turns the knobs of the four mantle lamps hanging from the ceiling, leaving them to go out slowly. He does not notice the dim light of the lantern as he shuts the café door. He remembers it suddenly when the screams ring out amid the gale, as the men from the lake charge like shooting stars through the streets. "I must have forgotten it, as usual. May God make it up to me," he says.

From the sides of the closed café door, the light of the lantern seeps out wan and pale amid the gloomy weather. The men from the lake head straight for it as soon as their feet touch firm ground. They may have already glimpsed it while riding the waves. Kicking the door again and again, they finally dislodge it with its hinges, hurl the chairs aside and start rummaging around.

Karawia waits until the downpours abate and daylight looms on the horizon. He hastens through the mud in the still stormy weather. Afifi will have preceded him to the shop as usual. Karawia glimpses him bent, lifting the door leaf from the mire. When he sees Karawia, Afifi wails,

"They took it! Oh, yes. They took it."

Karawia, who has not yet looked at his café, helps him prop the door leaf against the wall of the shop.

"A whole carton, Karawia. And that's apart from the boxes that were on the shelf."

As he rushes to the café, Karawia catches sight of the empty boxes of halvah afloat on the water that covers the empty space. Then he sees Afifi wade in to collect whatever his hands can reach, and hears him say plaintively, "They don't even wait till they get back. Oh, no. And they even throw away the empty boxes."

It seemed that it was on their way back that they broke into the shop, alerted to it by the smell of oil and paraffin that always emanates from the brick bench. Afifi chases the empty boxes until he is knee-deep in water. He stretches out the long stick as far as he can to catch the boxes, but he does not advance farther for fear of the ditches. When his pouched gallabiya fills up, he gazes at the boxes floating away. They bounce lightly on the water with the wind blowing in the direction of the lake. The gushing waves carry them back, and they settle not far away, where they shake, spin, and turn over.

"They who never throw away a thing—even a nail they pick up—now they throw the empty boxes."

He shoos away the boys who have sprung out of the darkness and rushed toward the empty boxes. They take no notice of his yelling and swim toward the boxes, and he swears at them.

On his way back, he stands with Karawia, contemplating

the café and the shop, which look like two dark apertures with their dislodged doors. The streets are empty and even the boys who had appeared so suddenly have just as suddenly disappeared. Gesturing to Afifi's laden lap, Karawia remarks, "And what would you do with these?"

"Whatever."

"You really should've left them to the boys."

"They already took enough."

The wind whistles inside the café, and the empty barrels in front of the shop shake.

"No one but us—just you and me," Karawia says.

"Yes."

"Every time."

Karawia blows his nose and curses. "And they are in their homes. What do they lose?"

"True. What do they lose?"

"And as if it's not enough, they've made us their laughingstock."

"Yes, I heard them."

"And if what's happened to us had happened to one of them . . . ?"

They help each other fix the two doors, shut them, and return.

A warm sun began to glow and the sky recovered its blue hue. White clouds scattered in the distance. Mild sea waves broke on the outlet of the channel, and silence reigned on the lake. Its small waves flowed to the channel, giving off a mellow purl as they parried the sea waves.

Early one morning they met in front of the café and set out to the lake. Karawia's brother-in-law was waiting for them in a boat. Afifi carried on his shoulder a carton with twenty boxes of halvah inside, while Karawia carried in his arms a plump black she-goat. They appeared to have settled everything. In the past few days they rarely parted. Whenever the customers in the café dwindled, Karawia gave a hand to Afifi in the shop, particularly on the days when he distributed the quotas of the ration books. He would stand behind the oil barrel with his sleeves rolled up, the measuring container in his hand, surrounded by the women. After closing the shop, Afifi would make his way behind the counter in the café, changing the water in the water-pipes, unblocking them and cleaning their coal-seats, then helping Karawia extinguish the mantle-lamps at the end of the evening.

They walked side by side to the shore.

"You should've brought them some tobacco. They all smoke," Karawia said.

Afifi scowled, and glanced at Karawia out of the corner of his eye, astonished by his sudden mirth. He pushed the goat away, then clasped it to his chest, abandoning his chin to its lips.

"The halvah will do. They want nothing else," Afifi said.

"Yes, that's true. They like it. They wouldn't have goats?"

"They have calves."

"And goats?"

"What would they do with them?"

"And what would they do with calves? And what would they do with anything, for that matter?"

They were drawing close to the shore. The boat swayed gently in the quiet waters. Karawia looked around for his relative, and spotted him concealed on the shore with only his turban showing. It appeared that he was answering a call of nature.

"Couldn't he have found another spot?" Afifi asked.

Karawia turned to him and said crossly, "This is as good as any other spot."

Afifi slowed down until Karawia was two steps ahead of him. Staring at the thick, dark back of his neck, he said, "I didn't know that you raised goats, Karawia."

Karawia's back froze and he turned around slowly. "Let me tell you something, Afifi, my friend. I know where the rest of the rationed oil goes when people get only half their quotas."

He suddenly dashed after the goat which had dropped from his arms during his outburst. They silently exchanged glances and Afifi turned back. Shortly afterwards Karawia followed him.

For months they did not talk, each avoiding the other. Karawia would send the café boy with the she-donkey to town to purchase his daily needs of water-pipe tobacco, paraffin, tea, and sugar. Having learned about their feud, the boy would stop the donkey laden with goods in the middle of the street in front of the shop and bend beneath it to fasten the saddle more tightly. The donkey would then part its hind legs and the boy would shout and pull it away as if to prevent it from peeing, though it would have already drenched the place, the spray bespattering the brick bench.

The fourth time the boy stopped the donkey, Afifi rushed out before he had bent beneath it, smacked him and showered blows on the beast, which sped away. He yelled out the threat that the next time it happened he would overturn the goods on the ground.

Whenever he glimpsed Karawia approaching, Afifi would push the door of the shop wide open and wait until he saw him walking past before spitting noisily to the side.

One day Karawia threw the tea dregs by the café wall facing the shop instead of in the hole on the beach. When he arrived in the morning, Afifi was taken aback by clouds of flies settling on the dregs. He opened the shop and told the customers who were waiting that he would not be long. Picking up the piece of wood with which he propped up the paraffin barrel, he rushed to the café. Karawia stepped out to him from behind the counter, but the customers stopped them before they could come to blows.

Their feud continued until the following gale. Afifi was wading through the water after the empty boxes. The weather was bleak and stormy, and the boxes had strayed far. The water reaching up to his knees, he stretched out his stick but only managed to catch three. He was startled to see a long reed stick stretching out nearby, and turning around, he saw Karawia. He would lift a box with the tip of the stick, raise it high dripping with water, then bring it down and throw it to Afifi. With his long stick he rapidly managed to pick up six boxes that had drifted away.

"I don't know what you do with them," Karawia said.

"They have their use."

The long stick caught up with a box that was bobbing with the wind toward the lake.

On their way back they paused to look at the apertures of the shop and the café. "Although this time I extinguished the lantern," Karawia said.

"Lantern or no lantern, they got into the habit and there's nothing to be done."

As they were fixing the doors, Karawia said, "You know, Afifi, that you won't find anyone but me when in need."

"True."

"People gloated when they saw us each in his corner. I'm sure their gossip reached you."

"It did."

"And what happens to us doesn't happen to any of them."

"Yes."

"Then let us put our trust in God and set out on our errand."

"As soon as the weather improves, we go."

"They'll be amazed when they see us before them."

"And how!"

"We see them and they see us."

"And we find out what all that is about."

They shut the doors of the café and the shop, and each headed home.

13

They met one morning a few days after the gale and walked to the shore. Afifi was carrying the halvah carton, Karawia the she-goat.

"Is it the same goat?" asked Afifi.

"The other one was black."

The goat in his arms was small and had white hair with a black lock on its forehead. They sat face to face in the boat, each with his load in front of him. The boat emerged into the open lake. Karawia's relative was rowing silently, with the corner of his shawl between his lips.

A large island came into view, so close that they could make out the smoke rising behind the few houses. Karawia's relative asked which island they wanted to go to. They exchanged glances. The island ahead looked familiar; they had often seen it while walking along the lake shore. "Any other island," Karawia said.

The blazing sun scorched their faces. The goat clung to Karawia's breast. He undid the light shawl from his head and covered the goat with it. His head in the wool skull cap looked small and round and was moist with perspiration. His eyes clouded over and he said, "The halvah will melt."

Afifi wiped off with his palm the sticky drops that were oozing from the sides of the carton. The heat grew more intense and their sweat had a salty tang. Each lifted the back of his gallabiya over his head like a tent.

As they advanced into the depths of the lake, the waters turned deep blue. Wavelets beat against the sides of the boat with a muffled sound.

"I've never been on the lake before," Karawia said.

"Neither have I."

"Even in my youth I never got near it."

"Me neither."

"The likes of us who've worked since childhood never got around."

"By God, you're right."

"Everyone else found the time to play. And what of us?"

"Even the nearby lake we saw only once a year, and from the shore."

A dark spot appeared on the horizon and the boat headed toward it. Feeling the small slippery rocks with their feet, they held onto each other's shoulders. Karawia's relative remained in the boat.

The island was a muddy, dark expanse without elevations. From where they stood they could see its other end. They walked for a short while and there was no creature in sight. Schools of Nile perch swam tranquilly in shallow ditches, half-full of water. Surveying the scene, Karawia said, "It's as if the water receded from it only a day or two ago."

He tightened his grip on the goat, which was trying to jump off his shoulder.

"And we may be the first to tread on it," Afifi said.

The lumps of mud that clung to their feet hindered their steps.

"Shall we go back?" Karawia asked.

"Yes, let's. Look at the bayad fish!"

"What a bayad!"

It was the biggest bayad they had seen in their lives,

swimming alone in a large pool. "What if we catch it?" Karawia said.

When it encountered their shadows on the water, the fish swam to one end of the pool then back again. It paused, spread out its fins, waved its tail, then darted away.

"If only we could catch it," Karawia said.

"And what would we do with it?"

"We could grill it."

"You'd need an oven—it's big."

"Take the goat."

He took off his gallabiya and put it on Afifi's shoulder. Though the water was shallow, he sank waist-deep into the sludge on the bottom. He was so terrified that he lost his voice. His arms flailed about and the water grew turbid around him. The bayad stopped away from the murky water and flared its fins in readiness. Karawia shifted his foot with difficulty and bent his torso until his face touched the water and he sneezed. He stared at the fish for a moment then worked himself out of the pool.

He left the island with sticky mud covering him up to the shoulders and crouched in the lake water by the boat. He took off his clothes, washed, and spread them out on the nearby rocks. His relative lit a fire between two stones and put the teakettle on it. Still crouching, Karawia crept until he was chest-deep in the water. When he gestured to Afifi to join him, he took off his clothes and sat beside Karawia in the water. Silence overcame them as they gazed at the blue water stretching in front of them.

Karawia said that if he had learned to swim when he was young he would have been swimming now.

Afifi said it was his first time.

They turned on their bellies and, resting on their elbows, let the water flow on their backs. Karawia wondered what Afifi did in his youth.

"Many things," Afifi said.

Grayish rocks littered the side of the island, with dense weed growth between them. "From place to place. At first, hand picking the cotton worm. Then, transplanting the rice seedlings into the basins. After that many shops opened in town. I was ten at the time," Afifi said.

"Which shop?"

"Abu Salem's carpentry."

Karawia laughed and hit the water with his foot. "I worked just opposite."

Afifi turned and stared into his face. Karawia said, "Yes. Mr. Shaker's shop. 'Lift the iron bars. Put down the iron bars.'"

"Oh, yes. Shaker."

"I once gave you two pieces of felafel and half a loaf of bread. Don't you remember?"

"Yes."

"You used to wear a striped cotton gallabiya with nothing underneath. It was too long for you so your mother tied it with a rope around your waist and hitched it up."

"It was my brother Ahmad's gallabiya."

"Its sagging front was always full—onions, scraps of bread, cheese crumbs, pebbles."

"Pebbles?"

"Yes. Small ones, round and colored."

"Now I remember. I used to play with them instead of marbles."

"And who'd play a game of pebble-marbles with you?"

"I used to play with them alone in the shop."

"And Abu Salem?"

"He'd be busy with the customers or in the street."

They dipped their faces in the water and, lying there, mimed the movements of swimmers.

"Oh, yes. And you?" Afifi said laughingly. "In cotton flannel pajama trousers with blue stripes and a long-sleeved undershirt."

"They were Mr. Abdel Dayem's trousers. He's a big-shot lawyer now. My mother used to wait until the school holidays started before going to his family. His mother never gave all of any set at once. First, she gave you the pajama trousers and said she'd look for the top. And for months she looked, and by the time she gave it to you, the trousers would have become frayed with holes like tunnels in them. Even with shoes."

"I never saw you wearing shoes."

"Yes. A single shoe. By the time she gave us its twin, the first had been lost."

"Your hair was auburn."

"Used to be. Let's see if you remember the day Abu Salem hit you and flung you out into the street. Yes, he lifted you by a leg and an arm and threw you out. The street was wet. You looked at your muddied gallabiya and started shrieking. Then Abu Salem threw a piece of wood at you to get you away from the shop. But you didn't even notice. You just stood there shrieking and not budging. Oh, yes. And your snot!"

"Anyone hearing you would think Amm Shaker never hit you."

"And how he hit me! Not once did he see me without smacking me on the back of my neck. 'Go find something to do.' And what could you do in an ironmonger's shop but carry the iron bars and put down the iron bars. But then you disappeared all of a sudden."

"Yes, I went away. My mother's cousin has a grocery shop. He took me in for several years."

"And then?"

"Then he became concerned about his daughters when he saw I'd grown up. And you?"

"Nothing much. After Shaker, I worked at a café in town."

When Karawia's relative signaled to them, they ran out of the water, covering their private parts with their hands. Standing in the shallow water by the boat they put on their clothes. They set out with the boat.

The second island they stopped at was broader. Taking a tour around it, they glimpsed three huts at one end on the edge of the slope. They had stopped the boat by a promontory jutting into the lake. The ground was damp and firm. Karawia walked carrying his goat, with Afifi behind him holding the halvah carton. Afifi had put a bundle of reeds on his shoulder under the carton, but oil still seeped from it onto his gallabiya, leaving a dark stain that grew larger.

They walked up a narrow track on the side of the island. The hewn steps had eroded edges. The island extended in front of them—wide, arid, and free of brush and reeds. Wavering a little, each moved his load to the other shoulder then proceeded. They saw many pegs and mud kilns with crumbling openings and ash heaped within to the side. There were remains of walls from which stones had been removed. They walked among them, stepping over the partitions between rooms.

"Deserted," Afifi murmured.

"Yes. They deserted them."

Afifi was rummaging with his foot amid the remains of the walls and Karawia asked what he was looking for.

"People sometimes leave things behind."

"Them? Leave things? They even took the bricks away."

"I don't mean things of value."

"What do you mean, then?"

"Well, things that tell you about them."

"Tell me? Why should I need to be told about them?"

"Because we don't know them."

"After all these years you don't know them?"

"You never know someone until you enter his home. Then everything about him becomes crystal clear."

"My, my. And where did you learn all this?"

"We learnt it from our parents."

"Afifi, nobody in this whole world knows you as well as I

do. Say you were looking for a ring, a spoon, the lid of a pot—that would sound more like it."

Karawia laughed and ran toward the three huts, which were crowded close together. Made of corrugated iron, their sides were corroded with rust. Their doors were closed with latches. Inside, they found old fishing nets, small square pieces of cork, bits of lead, and broken oars.

They stood in front of the huts, enjoying the shade and a cool breeze that was blowing forcefully. They looked at the lake at their feet, where small islands with dense vegetation appeared as dark spots floating on the blue water.

"You can't tell why they deserted them," Karawia said. "If it was for grass for the cattle, well it's all around them on the small islands."

"They don't settle for long anywhere."

"Yes. They build houses then pull them down."

"Karawia, let's go home."

"After all we've done, Afifi?"

"Time flies."

"Nothing annoys me as much as someone who goes halfway then says let's turn back."

Karawia's relative was asleep in the boat, having stuck the two oars on either side to secure it. They lunched from a parcel that was in the boat's hold—soft bread, cheese, and green broad beans. Karawia fed the goat straw and dry beans.

By the time they made for the open lake the sun had moved to the other side of the sky.

"We must be going the wrong way. I doubt if they sail for all these hours to reach us," Karawia said.

His relative turned the boat in a semi-circle and, rolling up his sleeves, said, "Let's try another direction." He'd never been on the lake before, he told them. He always casts his net not far from the shore. His catch, though never much, suffices. The lake appears easy for those who don't know it, he went on, but it's treacherous like all waters and many have lost their way on it and were rescued only by the people of the islands.

"Yes. More than one outlet links it with the sea. And there are whirlpools there the likes of which no one has seen. They could engulf a boat with all it carries."

He suddenly fell silent when he noticed their heads resting on their chests. Karawia was hugging the goat, Afifi leaning with his arm on the carton.

The din and shouting woke them. When Karawia saw his relative standing, he thought the boat was sinking, then he noticed the stones showering on them and heard Afifi groaning behind him. As the boat was approaching it had torn a fishing net spread underwater at the entrance of a small gulf. Nothing showed of it but pieces of cork hidden by the ripples. Children on the island were hurling stones at them, the wind carrying their shouts and curses to the open lake. Karawia's relative took off his clothes, jumped into the water, disentangled the prow from the net and pushed the boat back.

They moved away, heading for another side of the island. The boat came ashore by a muddy beach. The children were watching them from the island. Karawia's relative secured the boat to the beach and caught up with the others.

The ground was dry and level. Karawia widened his steps, followed by Afifi, the back of whose gallabiya had stiffened like taut leather. They were trailed by the naked children, holding green reeds. They passed a herd of calves grazing amid the green brush that grew denser on the slope of the island and a cement basin full of water with a flock of geese and ducks lying around it.

"At last!" Karawia exclaimed.

The houses at the other end were aligned in a bow-like row. There were nine similar houses, each consisting of two rooms with a walled-in courtyard. The lower half of the walls was of red brick, the upper part of mud brick daubed in mud. They had slanting roofs of corrugated iron. Seven old men emerged separately from the shade behind the houses. They were naked and skinny, with legs like dry sticks. Their private parts were covered with rags twined between their thighs. Karawia, suddenly exhilarated, rushed toward them with a smile. "Ah, father. It took us half a day to get to you."

One of them took a few steps forward, cocked his head and stared at Karawia. His drooping mouth was quivering. Karawia put his arm around him and walked him over to the others who were standing side by side. Their features were nearly identical: the many wrinkles on their faces, the small, restless eyes, the few hairs on their heads. Karawia let go of the old man and looked around. "Yes. And we never see you in town."

The old men looked at him then sat down on big, flat stones. Karawia sat on one of the other unoccupied stones in front of them, placing the goat between his legs. His relative and Afifi remained standing.

Old women swathed in black veils came out of the houses. They sat in the spaces between the stones behind the old men. Karawia gestured to his relative and Afifi to sit down. Afifi put the carton on his joined knees and dried his sweat with the end of his shawl.

"My friend Afifi. You must know him. His shop is the only one on the coast where you can find all you need, from a needle to a hook."

An old man got up, walked over to Karawia and, bending over, took the goat's face in his hand.

"Male?"

"No. It hasn't given birth yet. Take it. We brought it for you, and the halvah, too."

He stretched out his hand to the carton on Afifi's knees, but the old man was tottering back to the stone. "We brought it for you," Karawia said.

He carried the goat and put it in the old man's lap. The old man stared at its face and asked, "Male?"

"No, female."

Afifi put the carton of halvah in front of them, opened it and took out a box. Seeing the box in his hand, the boys leapt up shrieking and the women slipped out from among the stones. Each two boys took a box and ran off, while each woman took one. The women dipped their fingers into the halvah and fed the men. Then they turned away with what remained in the boxes and sat behind the men. With the tips of their tongues they caught the slivers of halvah around their mouths. An old man put out his stick and dragged an empty box to his side. Another, with flies buzzing around his face, got up and turned his back to them. He grasped the rag around his waist, which had loosened, revealing his lean behind. It was of a pale whitish hue, in contrast to his sun-scorched body. The old woman sitting behind him untied the rag from his waist, shook it out, and wrapped it up again between his thighs. Then he walked away followed by the old men, one after the other. "Where are they going?" muttered Karawia.

They walked feebly to the nearest house and disappeared inside. Clay dolls with straw hair hanging on the façades of houses swayed slightly in the breeze. The doors, which opened outwards, were ajar. They bore the imprints of large palms with outstretched fingers, the color of dry mud.

The women behind the stones were scrubbing the empty halvah boxes with earth. The children took the goat and set off to the basin. The old men returned, having washed the smears of halvah off their faces. They sat nearby, in front of fishing nets stretched between upright reed sticks. They started disentangling whatever threads had become knotted and picking out the weeds and shells that clung to the nets. Karawia glared angrily at them through the nets then turned to Afifi. Suddenly he shouted, "Where are the men?"

The old men behind the nets paid no attention to him. Their fingers moved between the holes swiftly and deftly. An old woman said, "Who are you asking about?"

"Your sons. Where are they?"

She gestured toward the open lake.

"And when will they come back?"

"When they come. If it's calves you want, we won't be selling before two months."

"We don't want calves."

The old woman turned and stared at him for a moment in silence, then said, "What do you want then?"

"We want them."

"Which one of them?"

"All of them."

"They won't come now."

"And when will they come?"

"They have no fixed time. They pass by from time to time."

"Pass? Don't they live here?"

"They live in their own houses."

"Where?"

She pointed to the open lake.

"Far?"

"Two or three islands away."

"I thought they lived with you."

"They pass by. They bring us water and everything else."

She scrutinized his face. "We have things to talk about with them," he explained.

"What do you want to talk about with them?"

Karawia looked at Afifi. The old woman shouted sharply, "What's going on? Every time I speak to you, you look at your friend. What's going on?"

Karawia pulled in his outstretched legs and said, "Nothing. It's all for the best."

An old woman was pounding something in a mortar, the rhythmic beats reverberating into the distance. The children darted shouting beside them then stopped on the edge of the slope and waved. Karawia and Afifi caught up with them. They glimpsed several boats with small unfurled sails, racing like the wind in the open lake. In a flash, they vanished behind a densely verdant island then reappeared. Their sails leaned to and fro, so inflated that the air seemed about to rip them. They continued their rapid passage until they disappeared amid the distant islands. The sun was about to set when they started back. Karawia and Afifi stretched out in the boat head to toe, and fell into a deep sleep, their heads swaying with the movements of the boat.

They came ashore after the evening prayer, and Karawia's relative headed home hauling his boat. They walked at a leisurely pace in the open space, kicking the thorn balls in their way. The shop and café in the distance were dark and the lights in the houses were turned off. There was a small light moving among them, as if someone was walking about with a lamp in hand.

14

For long days we sit on the doorsteps. Work is not always available in the town. It too has its own seasons, like everything around us. We make crates from palm stalks and earthenware pots, and try and find customers for them. We watch the passersby and sense the intense heat and the intense cold, and we see the two of them, Karawia and

Afifi, coming and going, venturing farther away, melting into the distant horizon. We forget them; then suddenly we find them in front of us. Something draws our attention to them, possibly the remarkable friendship that binds them and their tireless wanderings to and fro on the beach. They are like two children fooling around together, parting only when it is time to go to sleep. Neither feels embarrassed about stripping in front of the other when they go for a dip in the sea, choosing a distant spot on the beach. Afifi sits behind the counter in the café and Karawia sits in the shop seeing to the customers. They dress in the same fabric and hold identical dark brown canes, smooth and polished with a curved handle. They tell their wives to tend the shop and the café and set out. They have an amazing ability to walk for hours on end. And what are these long conversations about that never cease, as one leans on the other, his hand on his friend's shoulder, their quiet laughter carrying in the open space? They walk on the sea shore to the rock jetty, sit on its edge and dangle their feet in the water, the spray of the waves splashing them. They take along two fishing rods and spend half the day there, placing whatever fish they catch on reeds they have prepared beside them. When they have had their fill of angling they get up, paying no attention to the catch. They bought a small boat, in which they set out in the afternoon on the lake. They do not go far, but raise the oars and let the boat sway on the wavelets.

The shop and the café have become more prosperous. What with newcomers settling in the area and the laborers who have come to widen the reaches of the canal, their customers increased. Both the café and the shop were repainted, and Afifi's wife put up a fence of braided reed sticks and trellised it with palm stalks and jute. There she placed the barrels of oil and paraffin. After a fierce argument with his wife, Afifi secured the right to have lunch with Karawia at midday behind the trellis. She had received a kick from him that sent her tumbling from the brick bench of the shop into the street—and he was still in good health at the time. His friend Karawia was standing nearby, leaning on his stick, shaking his head regretfully. The two women would prepare the food for them, grumbling and calling on the Creator to take them both in one day.

On their return from their excursion on the beach at noontime, Karawia and Afifi would find their lunch, covered with an old gallabiya, ready for them behind the trellis. Then they would have tea and rest in two chairs amid the black barrels, watching the goings-on in the street through the gaps between the reeds, the passersby almost unaware of them.

Afifi's wife once listened to them after she had closed the door of the shop from within. She stood on a chair, looking through the bars of a small window at the top of the wall, from where she glimpsed their legs: Karawia had his crossed and was swinging his foot; her husband's leg was outstretched, his big toe jutting out into the street through the twined reeds.

Her husband said, "Karawia. We don't plan things carefully. But what if we did?"

"If we did, it would be hell, Afifi."

"Exactly. It'd be hell . . . like it is for most of the others."

"Oh, so many of the others."

The big toe was curled around the reed on which it rested, squeezing it. Knowing her husband's habits, she could tell from the movement of his toe the extent of the heaviness and bloating in his stomach.

"And even what we would achieve . . . " Afifi said.

"It would have no flavor."

"It would lose its juice."

"Like a dry corn stalk."

They fell silent. She waited for them to say something, but their silence lengthened. Quietly, she opened the door of the shop and saw them on the two chairs, their heads reclining.

Karawia's wife came after lunch and the two women took turns standing on the chair.

"Karawia, why do you think God created us?"

"For a purpose beyond our comprehension."

"Oh, yes—the talk we've been taught since childhood."

"That's all we were told."

"Millions of years, as they say. People are born, others die. A water-wheel turning and no one knowing the wisdom behind it. At times, thought draws me. It draws me and I find that I understand. Yes, I understand. Then, suddenly, understanding eludes me, as if a door has been closed."

"Anyone who tells you he understands it all is conning you."

"Then what's the answer?"

"What answer? The whole world is full of mysteries."

They were silent for such a long spell that the two women thought they had fallen asleep. Then Afifi's voice reached them.

"And what of the prophets?"

"What about them?"

"So many of them, I don't even know their names."

"Then learn them, Afifi."

"Do you know them?"

"I know six of them."

"They come to tell us to worship God. Well, I worship God."

"Others don't. Years pass, and people forget who created them, so He sends someone to remind them."

"I know all that already."

"Then what do you want?"

"And the crow, Afifi."

"Oh, but the crow."

"As much as people detest crows and think they bode ill, they're really very beautiful."

"Beautiful, and how!"

"Take their color. Black and navy blue. You don't find these colors in any other bird."

"And their beaks! True, the stuff they eat is disgusting. But their beaks . . . God be praised."

"I never hated them."

"Neither did I."

"I used to tie a crow's foot with a bit of rope. As it flew, I'd run along."

"And you went out into the open space?"

"Yes. And there in the open, you give it rope. It soars high and you, jumping over the puddles and ditches, feel you're flying with it. Have you ever seen a bird with such colors?"

"Neither a bird nor anything else."

"They're the two colors I like most. Even the gallabiyas I wear are either black or navy blue. And you?"

"White."

"White isn't a color."

"Of course it's a color, just like red and blue."

"I've never seen you in a white gallabiya."

"But I like white."

"Talk, talk. You like navy blue and black, just like me. All your gallabiyas. Oh, Afifi, if only you'd stayed in town and hadn't quit Abu Salem's shop, we'd have been the oldest of friends by now."

"And what difference would it have made?"

"A big difference. All that we're saying now we'd have said years ago."

"Karawia, what if we went again?"

"Yes, let's go. But wait till the goat has grown. In two months' time, we'll go. They won't elude us—where would they go? The lake, say what you will, is just a lake in the end. And the islands, no matter how numerous, will come to how many?"

"We pass by the old people?"

"And give them the halvah."

"And take another look at the bayad fish?"

"Ah, yes. The bayad."

"Maybe someone's caught it?"

"Who would?"

When the silence within the trellis lengthens, the two women sit down beside the chair and cry soundlessly.

"Where's it all going to end?"

"God have mercy upon us."

Months later, having apparently exhausted all possible topics of conversation, Karawia and Afifi took to wandering silently, each with his hands tucked under his armpits. Was it because of the biting chill in the air that they restricted their wanderings to midday hours? They now spent part of the evening in the café or behind the trellis, not a sound heard from within. It may have been their roaming and exhaustion that left that pallor and somberness on their faces, that distracted gaze. These were the signs we had seen on the faces of those who preceded them to perdition. It was but a small step, we said, before Karawia and Afifi joined them. Two or three would appear in town once every year, or so—always quiet, hiding in the doorways of houses whenever they glimpsed a brawl. They would walk incessantly, pause only for a moment when something caught their attention, then walk on. Each muttered to himself inaudibly in a heated argument that did not abate, his hands waving about questioningly. And the end came swiftly, always the same death, invariably.

For some reason they always ended their wanderings,

deep into the night, at the fields. They would go alone and stand apart at the corners of a plot of land, the tips of its low green vegetation swaying mildly. Hiding behind the fence of hemp stalks surrounding the plot, they would cock their heads as if listening for something, then steal glances toward the elevation where the track around the water-wheel is bare of trees, the darkness thinning over it. The one closest would start walking toward the wheel, followed by the two others. One of them would lie on the wooden wheel swinging his feet, and another would push him. The third would have straddled the scoop wheel, arms out-stretched, legs dangling to the side. The water-wheel turns and the scoop wheel dips him into the well. He emerges dripping as it turns. In the second cycle it emerges without him. And the water-wheel continues to turn. Its creaking reaches us in the last quarter of the night. We would go to the well whenever we noticed one of them had disappeared and haul out the bloated corpse.

We said it was only a matter of time before we saw Karawia and Afifi reach perdition. But that never happened. They escaped. They baffled us, were altogether beyond us. Their conversations almost petered out, and a deep silence reigned over them. They would content themselves with a glance exchanged while walking or amid the din of the customers in the café. Then they would smile and droop their eyelids, or they might frown and bow their heads as if they had already said all they wanted to say.

15

They left early one morning. Those who saw them assumed they were going on one of their cruises on the lake: they were carrying the same things they took every time. Afifi carried the two water jugs, Karawia the parcel of soft bread and filling.

The boat set out into the open lake, then they were out of sight.

Their wives awaited their return for lunch, which was ready behind the trellis and covered with the gallabiya. But they did not return. For days the whole community searched for them on the lake, and asked the people of the islands whenever they came for their supply of water, but no one had seen them. The search stopped a month after their departure and everyone forgot about them.

Five years will have elapsed before they reappear. Some of the locals, however, will have seen them before that. These were the ones who were dazzled by raids on the streets of the town and the settlement by the men from the lake and who would admiringly describe their swift running, their sudden disappearance, and their dexterous handling of the cudgels. From gale to gale they would await them behind windows and half-open doors. They said they had seen the two of them with the men from the lake, wearing the same rags and also carrying cudgels, though it did not occur to them that these were Afifi and Karawia. What caught their attention was the two men's sluggish, disordered running amid the heavy downpours, and their awkward grip on the cudgels. They also noticed that they were older than the others, with thick beards and bald heads, and that their movements were clumsy, so that they fell face down in the small puddles in their path. It was tempting to try and capture them, but as they hesitated briefly, the two men disappeared down the darkened alleyways. They chatted about them, laughing, after the gale. They would see them in the following gale, and still it would not occur to them that they are Karawia and Afifi. Later they would say that the faces looked familiar and that had they seen them close up, or even out of the rain, they would have recognized them. This they would say after Zakia talked.

A widow in her fifties whose husband had died long years before, Zakia lived with her mother-in-law in a small house close to Afifi's shop. In the days of the gale, she would open the door half-way and await the men from the lake returning from the town. They would break into the shop on their way back, and she would see them dash off into the open space carrying the boxes of halvah. She would wait for a little while until they had moved away, and before any of the neighbors, alerted by their din, peeped or came out, she would have bounded into the shop and snatched a piece of scented soap from a shelf she could not see in the dark but knew how to locate from having long stared at it. She had fourteen pieces of soap wrapped in their smooth, glossy paper, which she kept in an old gallabiya thrust into a corner of her clothes chest. She would bring them out when her mother-in-law was fast asleep or had gone out on a visit. She would smell them, feel the glossy paper, pass them over her neck and bosom, then put them back in the chest. Few in the settlement used this kind of soap. This she had deduced from the number of pieces on the shelf in the shop. She patiently awaited the death of the old woman, so that she could bathe with the scented soap without hearing an unwelcome comment. Every night, before falling asleep, she imagined the moment when the lush foam would cover her body and flow between her feet, its sharp scent suffusing the house. Two years will have passed since the disappearance of Karawia and Afifi when she stands at her half-open door watching the men from the lake returning from town.

There is mud on either side of the street, through which the water has carved its course. She hears the sound of their footfalls thumping in the flowing water. They flit past her door, break into the shop then rush off into the open space with the boxes of halvah, and disappear out of her sight. With her gallabiya rolled up to her knees, she darts out into the street. The door leaf is thrown aside. Stepping on it she bounds onto the threshold. She sees Afifi in front of her, emerging from the darkness of the shop. Her scream dies in her throat. Scampering into the street, she falls on her back. Unable to get up, she crawls in the mire and she sees him nearby, watching her. He is with another man. They scoop their hands into the halvah box and watch her. She goes on crawling, senses a wall, cleaves to it and runs home. She will have no doubts about it, no matter how long his beard is. It is that same face she has always detested. She keeps quiet about it, though, for who would believe her? Yet a dark fear oppresses her, so that when she hears what they say about two old men who accompany the men from the lake, she divulges her secret. It will astonish her that many believe her, as the features of the two men have always seemed familiar.

"And who could forget them?"

"Yes, it was Karawia," Zakia exclaims. "By the Prophet I didn't recognize him without the turban."

Afifi and Karawia's wives will stand up to all the talk, firm and sharp-tongued in their retorts. Afifi's wife will tell the women who have gathered on the doorstep of the shop, "If it is Afifi, as they say, then why didn't he enter his house? Has anyone angered him? And even if we did anger him, have you ever seen a man, whoever he may be, walk by his house like a stranger?"

"You're quite right. A woman, maybe. But a man, never. With his dying breath he calls for home."

And Afifi's wife says, "Let's assume it was Afifi and Karawia, as they say. Would they help break up the café and the shop? Never did we hear of a man who burns his own house."

"Anything but that."

The talk falls to whispers exchanged away from the two wives. Some will declare their intention to capture the two men in the next gale. But a gale will pass, and then another, and the two men do not come.

Afifi and Karawia's daughters will go out into the street. Three are of marrying age, two a little younger—the girls being their only offspring. Swathed in black veils, even the youngest, they walk to the shop. The flip-flops they wear make a clattering sound. They sit behind the trellis where Afifi and Karawia used to spend the midday hours. The passersby see them behind the braided reed sticks. They come in the morning and return at sunset. They do nothing, not even help Afifi's wife when the shop gets crowded. They sit still, with their eyes on the street, and exchange a few whispered words, rarely leaving the chairs lined along the fence. Their constant presence will do much to quell the nudges and insinuations and the children in front of the shop who mimic Afifi and Karawia's movements while walking or their posture when leaning on the cane.

On their second day out, the girls will linger for a while in front of Zakia's house. They will see her sitting on the doorstep looking at them with a smile, and there may be a hint of gloating in her smile. Before she realizes what is happening, she will have been flung into the street. She will fight them ferociously and the veil will slip off her henna-dyed hair, and despite her desperate resistance, they will manage to strip her, exposing her patched drawers for all to see. They leave her tattered in the middle of the street, gathering herself and slapping her own face in shame, and proceed to the trellis at their usual pace.

The two families will come together in Karawia's house, the larger of the two. The girls will disappear home once again and the locals will go back to their former ways, remembering nothing of the whole episode except the rough beating Zakia got and her patched drawers.

The gale looms on the horizon. The two women close the

café and the shop and go down the dark street. The wind is whistling, the doors and windows shaking at its impact.

"You know what I'm afraid of?" Afifi's wife whispers.

"I know."

"If what Zakia saw . . . "

"Yes."

"Do you believe her?"

"And why shouldn't I?"

"Me too."

They slow down as they draw close to the house and the girls' laughter reaches them. Karawia's wife says, "Suppose they capture them as they intend?"

"It would be better."

Karawia's wife stops and stares at her.

"And what if they take it into their heads to come by the sea route as some do!" Afifi's wife exclaims.

"Oh, my God!"

They exchange glances silently then Afifi's wife says, "Even if they've learnt how to swim over there!"

They pause for a moment, staring dejectedly at the lit window of the house.

They will keep their fears to themselves, whispering about them only when out of earshot. More than anything else, it will terrify them that the women who go out to the shore during the gale might find their two bodies naked, peer at their private parts, and perhaps even poke them with their sticks as they do with the other corpses.

Afifi's wife lowers her eyes. She blushes and says hoarsely, "No. That would be shameful."

"Yes. Shameful."

More than one gale will have passed without the sea spewing any corpses, but this will not allay their fears. They will await the gale and go out, each with a folded sheet tucked under her arm. They avoid the open space in front of the channel where the women usually gather before going to the shore, and head in the opposite direction. They proceed amid the sand dunes in a slanting line that takes them to the rocks of the seashore. Without astonishment they will mention that they have never been out to the shore before. They will be awe-struck by the violent sea, the clamorous roar, and the gray mountainous waves that loom close, and they will stand there shivering. The stormy wind all but sweeps them off their feet. They move, holding each other's hands, treading cautiously, away from the water. Their feet sink into the wet sand and the sharp spray stings their faces. Unaware of the ditches full of water, they trip and fall. Although it is dark, they can make out what is afloat on the nearby waters. They cross the shore from the rocks, moving closer to the channel. The inundated space in front of the houses comes into view. They climb up the sand dunes and head back.

They will continue to go out with every gale, driven by an apprehension that does not abate. Five years will have elapsed since the departure of the two men, and having in vain watched for their arrival with the men from the lake, the inhabitants of the area will have forgotten them. They will start doubting what they have seen, saying that they must have been mistaken, amid the rain and the dark streets, and had it not been for what Zakia said, their suspicions would never have turned to them.

The two women go out in the stormy weather and head for the shore.

"My heart tells me this will be the gale," Afifi's wife says.

"May God have mercy upon us."

They avoid the gushing water, each with a stick in hand with which to circumvent the hidden ditches. Glimpsing a hollow in the sand where the water has gathered into a small puddle, they turn to detour around it. Afifi's wife stops and gazes into the puddle. Standing behind her, Karawia's wife whispers, "Them?"

"Them."

The two bodies float apart, each sticking to one side of the puddle, shaking with the ripples. The rags they wear are rolled back to the shoulders. The women drag them one after the other and lay them on the dry sand. They empty their mouths of weeds, clean their noses and ears and wrap their naked bodies in the two sheets. Then they sit by their heads.

And They Left

16

They had come before. They pitched tents on the shore and constructed a concrete dam on the mouth of the channel, the side that gives onto the sea. A few days later they constructed another dam behind it, a step away. With parted legs, the boys would walk on the dams to the other bank. And they left.

Then they returned. They pitched their tents for one day and burned the grass and weeds on the banks of the channel and along the shore of the lake. The fire left dark patches that continued to spout smoke for two days. Turbulent sea waves lashed violently at the dam, then retreated foaming. The waves came successively, the sound of their thumping reverberating deep into the lake. Sometimes they slackened, flowing languidly in front of the dam, lapping it with a hissing sound before withdrawing.

The channel grew shallow, its waters stagnant. Its sides were laid bare, with many clefts, crevices, and black rocks exposed. A putrid odor emanated from the channel as it filled with algae that the lake tossed in from time to time.

Once again we saw the tents pitched at the rocks on the

seashore. Concrete columns were sprouting there, away from our sight. At first we saw them as small as pegs. Then they grew, towered high and were crossed by beams. They were like skeletons around which the bulldozers hurtled. We waited for the spaces between them to fill so they would acquire shape.

We would sit in the afternoons in front of the houses gazing at them, watching their colossal shadows extend far over the shore. They were creeping toward us, preceded by the bulldozers.

One day a black boat came ashore at the mouth of the channel. A woman leaning on a stick stepped down from it, followed by two men. They walked along the bank of the channel then sat down there, watching the bulldozers and the heavy dust they stirred. They sat there for almost an hour then started digging. They brought out bones they put in a sack and a skull the woman wiped of dust with the hem of her gallabiya. They took turns looking at it before putting it in the sack. They brought out a chest but did not open it. They leveled the hole and walked back carrying the sack and the chest. Before getting into the boat, the woman turned and pointed with her stick at the houses, and the two men looked in the direction to which she had pointed.

And the boat sailed off into the open lake.

Modern Arabic Literature
from the American University in Cairo Press

Ibrahim Abdel Meguid *Birds of Amber* • *Distant Train*
No One Sleeps in Alexandria • *The Other Place*
Yahya Taher Abdullah *The Collar and the Bracelet* • *The Mountain of Green Tea*
Leila Abouzeid *The Last Chapter*
Hamdi Abu Golayyel *Thieves in Retirement*
Yusuf Abu Rayya *Wedding Night*
Ahmed Alaidy *Being Abbas el Abd*
Idris Ali *Dongola* • *Poor*
Radwa Ashour *Granada*
Ibrahim Aslan *The Heron* • *Nile Sparrows*
Alaa Al Aswany *Chicago* • *The Yacoubian Building*
Fadhil al-Azzawi *Cell Block Five* • *The Last of the Angels*
Liana Badr *The Eye of the Mirror*
Hala El Badry *A Certain Woman* • *Muntaha*
Salwa Bakr *The Golden Chariot* • *The Man from Bashmour* • *The Wiles of Men*
Halim Barakat *The Crane*
Hoda Barakat *Disciples of Passion* • *The Tiller of Waters*
Mourid Barghouti *I Saw Ramallah*
Mohamed El-Bisatie *Clamor of the Lake* • *Houses Behind the Trees* • *Hunger*
A Last Glass of Tea • *Over the Bridge*
Mansoura Ez Eldin *Maryam's Maze*
Ibrahim Farghali *The Smiles of the Saints*
Hamdy el-Gazzar *Black Magic*
Tawfiq al-Hakim *The Essential Tawfiq al-Hakim*
Abdelilah Hamdouchi *The Final Bet*
Fathy Ghanem *The Man Who Lost His Shadow*
Randa Ghazy *Dreaming of Palestine*
Gamal al-Ghitani *Pyramid Texts* • *The Zafarani Files* • *Zayni Barakat*
Yahya Hakki *The Lamp of Umm Hashim*
Bensalem Himmich *The Polymath* • *The Theocrat*
Taha Hussein *The Days* • *A Man of Letters* • *The Sufferers*
Sonallah Ibrahim *Cairo: From Edge to Edge* • *The Committee* • *Zaat*
Yusuf Idris *City of Love and Ashes*
Denys Johnson-Davies *The AUC Press Book of Modern Arabic Literature*
In a Fertile Desert: Modern Writing from the United Arab Emirates
Under the Naked Sky: Short Stories from the Arab World
Said al-Kafrawi *The Hill of Gypsies*

Sahar Khalifeh *The End of Spring*
The Image, the Icon, and the Covenant • *The Inheritance*
Edwar al-Kharrat *Rama and the Dragon* • *Stones of Bobello*
Betool Khedairi *Absent*
Mohammed Khudayyir *Basrayatha*
Ibrahim al-Koni *Anubis* • *Gold Dust* • *The Seven Veils of Seth*
Naguib Mahfouz *Adrift on the Nile* • *Akhenaten: Dweller in Truth*
Arabian Nights and Days • *Autumn Quail* • *The Beggar*
The Beginning and the End • *Cairo Modern*
The Cairo Trilogy: Palace Walk, Palace of Desire, Sugar Street
Children of the Alley • *The Day the Leader Was Killed*
The Dreams • *Dreams of Departure* • *Echoes of an Autobiography*
The Harafish • *The Journey of Ibn Fattouma* • *Karnak Café*
Khan al-Khalili • *Khufu's Wisdom* • *Life's Wisdom* • *Midaq Alley* • *Miramar*
Mirrors • *Morning and Evening Talk* • *Naguib Mahfouz at Sidi Gaber*
Respected Sir • *Rhadopis of Nubia* • *The Search*
The Seventh Heaven • *Thebes at War* • *The Thief and the Dogs*
The Time and the Place • *Voices from the Other World* • *Wedding Song*
Mohamed Makhzangi *Memories of a Meltdown*
Alia Mamdouh *The Loved Ones* • *Naphtalene*
Selim Matar *The Woman of the Flask*
Ibrahim al-Mazini *Ten Again*
Yousef Al-Mohaimeed *Wolves of the Crescent Moon*
Ahlam Mosteghanemi *Chaos of the Senses* • *Memory in the Flesh*
Mohamed Mustagab *Tales from Dayrut*
Buthaina Al Nasiri *Final Night*
Ibrahim Nasrallah *Inside the Night*
Haggag Hassan Oddoul *Nights of Musk*
Mohamed Mansi Qandil *Moon over Samarqand*
Abd al-Hakim Qasim *Rites of Assent*
Somaya Ramadan *Leaves of Narcissus*
Lenin El-Ramly *In Plain Arabic*
Ghada Samman *The Night of the First Billion*
Rafik Schami *Damascus Nights*
Khairy Shalaby *The Lodging House*
Miral al-Tahawy *Blue Aubergine* • *Gazelle Tracks* • *The Tent*
Bahaa Taher *As Doha Said* • *Love in Exile*
Fuad al-Takarli *The Long Way Back*
M.M. Tawfik *Murder in the Tower of Happiness*
Mahmoud Al-Wardani *Heads Ripe for Plucking*
Latifa al-Zayyat *The Open Door*